Banged

Blue Collar Bad Boys, Volume 9

Brill Harper

Published by Brill Harper, 2018.

This is a work of fiction. Similarities to real people, places, or events are entirely coincidental.

BANGED

First edition. March 7, 2018.

Copyright © 2018 Brill Harper.

ISBN: 979-8223419136

Written by Brill Harper.

About this Book

He's a warrior with no battle. A cop with no bad guy. A man with no purpose.

WHEN MY BEST FRIEND and ERU partner was blown up by a bomb I should have been able to defuse, I vowed to never let anyone get that close again. I'm just drifting through life, and that's okay with me. If I can't feel, I can't hurt.

Until I meet my neighbor.

I've been doing my best to avoid the too-pretty pregnant girl next door. She stirs too many things inside me I have no business feeling. She's too young, too fresh, too pregnant with someone else's kid for me to be fantasizing about.

Until the day I can't ignore her anymore.

Hillary is a born caretaker, but nobody takes care of her. She's alone in the world, but not for much longer, not with the way that baby dances in her belly. She's all the things I try to stay away from—optimistic, uncommonly sweet, and oh, yeah, she's somehow still a virgin.

Author's Confession: You read that right. She's a pregnant virgin. I probably don't need to say anything else to get you to one-click at this point, but I'll go ahead and tell you the bomb technician will make your heart go BOOM. He's the alpha caretaker you want guarding your six. And your nine...

Chapter One

Mac

I REALLY HATE THIS coffee shop.

The darkest corner I could find is still lit up like they're using stadium lights, and the speakers placed every two feet are blaring annoyingly spirited pop music of the boy band variety. The air even tastes sweet, like bubblegum. It's like Whoville and all the noise, noise, noise. Fuck.

The barista at the counter even looks like Cindy Lou Who with her shiny blonde hair braided up and her too tight T-shirt showing too much skin. Maybe some men like that. Maybe she gets great tips. But she does nothing for me other than make me want to suggest she put on a sweater and get her homework done.

The music in here jangles my nerves, but so do the clattering dishes, the clinking spoons, the scrape of metal against metal. My blood pressure is rising, the thumping in my head getting louder and louder. A cash register dings and the vein in my temple throbs.

Hold it together, Stryker.

I sip at my acrid, burnt coffee, and it scalds the inside of my mouth.

That quiet spot inside my head that used to make my job dismantling explosives possible seems to have disappeared, leaving me like this—always one step from losing my shit. My hand throbs, a reminder of why I'm sitting here instead of at the station or out on a call. I could probably hide the stuff going on in my head if I had to, but nobody is letting me go back to work until my hand heals, something physical therapy doesn't seem to be doing.

I frown into my cup. If I have to be at a coffee shop instead of the cop shop, I wish I were at Old Joe's instead. Old Joe's feels more like a pub, only instead of booze they serve smooth coffee and normal looking desserts that taste like food and not plastic and saccharin. But now I come here because *she* had to ruin it all.

I don't know her name. She's pretty. She's smiley. She's pregnant.

And she's my neighbor.

The last day I stepped foot in Old Joe's, I took one look at her behind the counter, that sunny smile and pretty little dimple, her dark chin-length hair the same shade as her deep brown eyes, and I turned around and never went back. It's hard enough to avoid her in the hallway outside our apartments, I don't need to run into her every day over my coffee. Then she'd start talking to me. Asking me questions. Getting to know me. Then she'd expect that we chat at the mailbox. Maybe gossip about the neighbor down the hall who entertains an awful lot of men in her apartment when her husband is at work. Then comes "borrowing a cup of sugar" or "I made extra lasagna and brought you a plate."

No. Thank. You.

For one thing, I don't want to be friendly with anyone. It's not just her, but she's worse. She's the kind of person that you can tell is genuinely nice. Good inside. Not faking it like most of us. Ten years on the police force and I can tell you I know for certain there are more assholes like me in the world than honestly nice human beings like her.

But the other thing that keeps me far, far away from the girl next door is I want to fuck her.

Bad.

She's deliciously round. Fertile. It shouldn't even be sexy. I've never been turned on by a pregnant woman before.

But being someone's mother means she'd best stay away from the likes of me. Not only am I not interested in commitment or family, but I'm a fucking mess. Nobody deserves to be saddled with me, but especially not someone responsible for another human life.

I've never seen a baby daddy hanging around, but he's out there somewhere. He should be home with her. Keeping guys like me from drooling all over the mother of his kid. The fantasies I have make me feel dirty. Well, after I come, I feel dirty. While I'm stroking to the thought of her, I feel fucking fantastic. The things I want to do to that woman are not legal in some states.

Better change the direction of my thoughts. The last thing I need is a hard-on when my boss gets over here.

Captain Albright weaves around the long line at the cash register and toward my table. I stand, offering him my left hand rather than my right now that it's so messed up.

We catch some startled stares from the Abercrombie & Fitch crowd around us. We don't exactly fit in with the "One Direction is the best band ever" patrons. Cap isn't a small man, and we're evenly matched in height, though he's got about forty pounds on me. Most of the guys on my ERU squad are big. It seems to go with the territory. Though Cafferty, the one handling the bombs that used to go to me, is about 5'9" and wiry as fuck. He's the dude we always send into crawlspaces first.

After shaking my hand, Cap pulls me into a bear hug and slaps my back. "Stryker, what's good here?"

"Bottled water," I answer and slap him back.

He laughs and scans the chalkboard with specials written on it in fat bubble letters. "I like that sweet drink, right? What is it called?"

"Mocha, sir. I already ordered you one. They said they'd bring it to the table." I signal to Cindy Lou Who that I'm ready for that drink, and we sit in the hard plastic chairs the colors of a neon nightmare.

"How are you doing, son? I read the most recent report on your hand this morning."

I blow out a frustrated breath. "I need to come back to work. I'm going crazy, Cap."

His eyes are warm, but his expression resigned. "You're not logging in all your psych meetings." His coffee arrives in the hands of a different young woman who shoots me an appreciative glance. At least she looks a couple years older than the blonde, but I'm still not interested. "Thank you," Cap says, offering another tip for the delivery to the table.

I'd already added a tip, but I don't begrudge her getting more. It gives me a few more seconds of not hearing the bad news anyway. When she leaves, my time is up.

Cap sighs. "I can't bring you back until both your doctors agree, and that psychologist will never clear you unless you do the time."

I was afraid of that. "I'll start going to the group meetings again. I just...hate it." I can't decide which is worse—the group sessions or the one-on-ones with my psych doc. That fucker sort of makes me want to punch things more when I'm inside his office than I do outside of it.

"None of those cops want to be there, but there's no shame in it. We have to lean on each other sometimes, Stryker. Everyone in that meeting is dealing with similar shit."

I nod. The guys in the group are not the problem. I can relate to all of them. Two of the guys also lost their partners on the job like I did. There's no manual telling you how to deal with that. Well, there is. There's a manual for everything at the police department. Just not a useful one.

Ricky was more than my partner on the squad; he was my best friend. Every night, I relive his last moments. Every day, I walk around feeling like a ghost.

It should have been me. I wish it had been me.

Cap fills me in on some gossip from our unit. I miss the ERU. Cafferty can handle explosives as well as I could, so the team will be okay without me. But I'm not sure I'm okay without the team. I can't defuse a bomb with a fucked-up hand, though. I miss my family, my squad, but I have to wonder if I'm actually any good to them at all anymore.

I THINK ABOUT IT DURING the walk home. Maybe it's time to rethink careers. But shit, what does a bomb guy do if he's not defusing bombs? I've been a cop since I graduated high school, in some form or another.

Out of habit, I check the entryway of my building for anything that seems out of the ordinary. There never is. It's a good neighborhood, and I'm not the only cop living in it. I've lived here long enough that I've already mentally placed all the explosives in the places I'd hide them if I were the bad guy. I guess it's part of the job, always expecting the worst. It doesn't help. Surprises still happen, and they still suck. But everywhere I go, I'm hiding bombs in my head and checking to make sure they aren't there.

It isn't until I round the stairwell on my floor that I hear *her*. My neighbor. I pause. Maybe she hasn't sensed me yet, and I can turn around and wait for her to get inside her own apartment. No awkward hellos necessary.

Only she's not standing at her door. She's sitting on the floor, slumped against the wall, and fuck me, she's crying.

I'm a tough man. As a cop I've seen things, done things, that most people can't imagine in their worst nightmares. I'm confronted with the worst of the human condition regularly. I've witnessed utter hopelessness, unparalleled anger, and unspeakable violence. And I face it and do my job.

But this one woman, crying in the hall, fucking undoes everything inside me. Shit. Shit. Shit.

I make noise as I walk down the hall so it doesn't seem like I'm sneaking up on her. She doesn't seem to notice or stop crying. Shit.

"Ma'am?"

She gasps and looks up, her lip and chin trembling, but it's the ashen color of her face that worries me the most.

With arms wide so she can see I'm not holding a weapon, I use the voice I've had to practice on victims of accidents and crimes too many times. It's deep, slow, relaxed. "I'm sorry to startle you. I live next door. My name is Mac. MacKenzie Stryker. I'm a cop." I show her my badge.

She nods quickly, faking a casual air. "I've seen you before." The color of her face changes from gray to pink. "I'm Hillary Bloom."

"Hillary, can you tell me what's wrong?"

She gifts me with a watery smile and then bursts into uncontrollable sobs once again.

Not sure if I should, I touch her arm gently. "Please don't cry."

That apparently sets her off a little more, and she tries to breathe but only manages hiccups. I lean into her, registering the scent of coffee and something buttery that she must have carried home on her from her shift at Old Joe's. I fold around her gently. I haven't comforted anyone in a long time. The last woman I hugged was Ricky's wife at his funeral, and I'm sure I offered her no consolation or comfort at the time.

Hillary, though, slows her hiccupping. She's stuttering something that sounds like "I'm sorry" and "I'm so embarrassed."

I rub her back and resist the urge to kiss her head. "Can you tell me what's wrong?" *Please. I need to fix it.* I can't stand the tears, they're killing me.

She pulls back and looks at me through those damp and overly bright eyes. "How much time do you have?"

No one is more surprised by the laugh that chuffs out of me than I am. "My schedule is clear for a bit." She shakes her head like she's talking herself out of telling me. "Hillary..."

"I have to pee."

Well, okay. That's normal for a pregnant woman, I guess.

"But I've lost my keys." Her voice tightens. "And I can't get in to my apartment and," her face scrunches up and her chin trembles, "and I have to pee."

"Okay—"

Before I can give her a solution, she continues. "And also, I've had a really long day. All my days are long right now on account of being so uncomfortable, but it's harder at work, and today was harder than usual, and I spilled the butterscotch syrup all over myself so I've been sticky and gross for hours, and I just want to get in my apartment—" She pauses for a deep breath then continues, "I need to clean up and pee and put my feet up because I have no ankles anymore."

She pauses. Finally. But I'm lost. "What?"

"Nobody told me being pregnant was going to steal my ankles, but they're gone. And I got so frustrated when I couldn't find my keys that I slid to the floor to have a good cry. I do that a lot—cry, not slide to the floor, because now that I'm down here, I can't get up. And all I want is to pee and clean up and put my feet up and I need to eat some mac-n-cheese or I'll probably die or something equally dramatic."

"Mac-n-cheese," I repeat.

Jesus. She's fucking adorable. Her dark lashes are damp with tears, and her top lip is shaped like the bow on a present. I want to press a kiss there. I need to get my head back in the game because she's still talking. Rambling really, but I don't mind because the sound of her voice makes me feel lighter inside.

Jesus, this woman.

"I know it's not great for the baby, but I crave it all the time. And it has the be the blue box because the store brand..." There goes that chin. The store brand of macaroni makes her cry, I guess. "So, now I'm stuck on the floor like a beached whale. Which is not very attractive or very comfortable. And I was sitting here crying, and I realized that I have to raise this baby alone. I mean, I knew that, but it just really started sinking in how hard it's going to be. And I don't mean to complain, but it's kind of scary. Being alone. And who is going to date me? I'm pregnant with another man's kid and then when I'm not, I'll be too busy raising a baby alone to date anyone ever again and then I'll be too old, which means..." She shudders on a long, ragged inhale. "Which means I'm going to die a virgin."

Chapter Two

Hillary

I CLAP MY HAND OVER my mouth in a belated attempt to hold back the words spewing from me, but it's too late.

Much, much too late. Oh my God.

Not *once* in all the pregnancy books I've read have they mentioned uncontrollable speech as a pregnancy symptom. Not in any trimester. But I have no other plausible excuse for the verbal assault I just committed on the man who lives next door to me.

It figures that I'd finally meet him when I'm beached, bloated, snot-filled, and have emotional Tourette's. That's pretty much how life goes these days for me.

Mac Stryker is the literal embodiment of virile man with a capital V. I know I'm extra horny from all the hormones, yet another of life's little jokes for me, but honestly, if I weren't already pregnant I'd be worried that just his proximity would do it.

He smells like spearmint and spice, and I wonder if he'd let me take a nap in his sheets because I have a feeling I'd finally sleep well for a change if I were surrounded by his scent. I should be careful what I wonder. I'm liable to say it out loud. I'm sure the last thing this hot guy wants is the mental image of me rolling around in his sheets.

To his credit, he doesn't outwardly react to my incoherent (I hope) rambling. "Okay, Hillary. Let's tackle this one problem at a time. The way I see it, getting into your apartment would solve several of your problems simultaneously, so that's our first step."

I nod, resigned to a bill from a locksmith I can ill afford.

Mac stands, and my gaze follows his rise all the way up. He's tall and dense with hard-packed muscle. God. More granite than man, he's robust and sturdy, nothing can knock him down. What is that like? Knowing you can just buffet whatever winds life throws at you by standing still. Since I got preggo, I've felt insecure. It was hard enough taking care of myself when I was alone, but now I'm supposed to shelter this tiny human inside me from everything scary and dangerous. Why didn't God make mothers the ones with all the upper body strength instead of men? We need it more.

He pulls something out of his pocket and goes to my door, inserting a silver object into the handle.

"What are you doing? Are you...are you breaking into my apartment?"

He doesn't turn, which is not a problem. The view of his backside is okay fine with me. His ass is a work of art encased in tight blue jeans. Perfectly proportioned tight, round spheres. "Yep."

"I thought you said you were a cop? What kind of cop knows how to break into apartments?" And carries the tools to do it?

"The resourceful kind," he answers, he looks over his shoulder with a wolfish grin. "I find it's best to know what the perps can do and how they do it if I want to stop them. Also, as a cop, I have to tell you that your door isn't very secure, and you need better locks. The kind not so easy to break."

He jiggles the handle, and I hear a pop just before the door opens. My relief is short-lived. I still can't get off the floor. And no, I do not want his help. My God. This is humiliating.

"You're mentally trying to figure out which yoga position will get you off the ground, Hillary. I can see it."

The blush is hot and fierce as it spreads from my scalp to my toes. The only thing worse than trying to stand in front of this hot guy is not standing up in time and wetting myself. I get to my hands and knees, but the hot ball of tears in my throat won't go back down. Shit. I'm going to cry again.

"Hey," his warm voice blankets me. He's down on the floor at face level. "I'm going to help you get up, okay?"

"I can do it." I totally can't. There's no way I can bend the laws of physics, but maybe I can just roll into my apartment. The baby crane-kicks me in the bladder. I wince but manage not to swear. I've been working on it. I don't want to swear at my kid when it comes out, so I try not to swear at it while it's cooking either. But man. Sometimes Little Bloomer makes it difficult. That was some kick. "I can do it," I repeat.

"Hillary, I'm a trained professional."

"Yeah? Cops train for this? Where, the zoo? You guys work with the elephants and walruses?"

He makes this noise that's a cross between a heavy sigh and an almost laugh. "Anyone ever tell you that you tend to exaggerate? I'm a big strong man, Hillary. I can handle this."

I blow out a breath and allow him to help me up slowly. He really is a big strong man. He helps me find my center of gravity and Bloomer starts rolling under his hand. Mac stops all movement, and his eyes get big. "Was that the baby?"

"Yeah, he or she is really active today." The baby rolls again. "You ever felt a baby kick before?"

Mac shakes his head. I have to say he looks a little pale. I move his hand an inch and place mine over it, waiting for another movement. When it happens, Mac's face transforms into the smile of a kid who just saw a bike under the Christmas tree.

"Holy shit!"

"Yeah," I answer with a laugh. "It's pretty crazy, right?"

He puts his other huge paw on my stomach and waits for another one. It's like watching for the dice to stop rolling at a roulette table.

We're hushed, expectant. Bam! He laughs. It's hearty and rich, and my heart flips in tandem with my baby at the sound of it.

"That is amazing." He ushers me into my own apartment, one hand still on my belly. "Does it hurt?"

"Not usually. Sometimes. The first time Bloomer moved, I thought I had some kind of small rodent trapped in my shirt. I totally freaked out."

Mac closes the door behind us and puts my purse on the couch. "I'm going to take some pictures of your door so I know what kind of hardware we need to shore it up."

"Mac, I can't afford—"

"The landlord owes me a favor. I'll make sure he covers the cost."

I don't believe that for a minute. The landlord doesn't fix shit in this building, but I'm not going to argue on a full bladder.

I already have to face a virgin birth, I'm not going to add "also peed her pants in front of her neighbor" to my headstone.

Mac

WHILE HILLARY IS IN the bathroom, I figure the smartest move I can make is start some water boiling for her macaroni. I get out a blue box of Kraft and eye it suspiciously. Better make it two. She was pretty intense out in the hall.

I don't know much about pregnant women, though I did have training for emergency deliveries, but I do understand that you can't be pregnant and a virgin at the same time. I'm hoping maybe it's just that her blood sugar dropped too low and she doesn't *really* believe she's like Mary, the mother of God. I made the choice not to question her when she was stuck on the floor, and I think it was the right one, but fuck if I'm not curious. Maybe I heard her wrong. There was a lot of information to parse out of all that rambling.

I think I've taken care of the most pressing issues: she's off the floor, in her apartment, relieving her bladder, and going to eat macaroni soon.

Her apartment is warm and welcoming. Plants hanging from hooks, a patchwork quilt folded over the back of a chair, pillows on the floor and on the couch. My apartment is the mirror image of hers, but a lot less cozy. Though my TV is better. Much better. That and a recliner are all I have in the living room. What else does a single guy need though?

Apparently single women need more seating, more color, more comfort, and less screen size.

She's a reader. Books are stacked haphazardly on the coffee table and more fill the bookshelves against the wall. It looks like a mix of fiction and art books, but also plenty of books about pregnancy and babies. I scan for photos or evidence of a baby daddy, but the living room area and kitchen don't offer me any more clues. It's not my business, but I'm curious.

The water is boiling when I add the pasta and catch sight of movement across the room.

"You're cooking for me?"

She's fucking beautiful. She's changed her clothes; the tight T-shirt stretches over her baby bump and emphasizes her abundant curves. Her pants are just pajama pants with cats on them, but something about her casual attire just slays me. Like I'm in some private inner sanctum where I get to see who she is when she's not out in the world. Her face is freshly washed of tear tracks and her hair is down and frames her face.

"You feeling better?" I ask dumbly. I don't know what else to say. The things that are bubbling up in my throat are words that don't make sense or would be inappropriate to say.

Beautiful.

Goddess.

I want to make you come.

See? Inappropriate.

But there's more. Things about staying, about commitment, about forever and never feeling like this before.

It's all too much. My chest tightens, my ribs crushed by a boa constrictor of unrelieved feelings. Feelings I've never experienced before and have no right to now.

"Yes, I feel better. Thank you for the rescue." I shouldn't be turned on by the tiny waddle as she crosses the room. "You don't have to cook for me. You've already helped me so much today."

I grunt—a standard reply that I fall back on to keep people from getting too close. Nobody wants to get near a grumpy bastard, after all.

There's a surprised wistfulness in her eyes, but she blinks it back. "You could be an ax murderer, but I'd let you stay if you made me mac-n-cheese. I probably shouldn't tell that to a cop, but there you go. I'm not above aiding and abetting for cheap pasta and processed cheese."

"Then sit."

She eases onto the bar stool. "Just what kind of cop are you, Stryker?"

"ERU."

Her mouth falls open. "Really? That's...wow. That's kind of crazy. I never knew an ERU officer before."

"Not everyone knows what the ERU does."

"Well, I don't even know what the initials stand for, but I know you guys are the ones they call for the big stuff. At least I only ever hear *ERU* on the news when the shit hits the fan."

"Emergency Response Unit. My specialty is...was...bomb tech."

Her hand flies to her throat. "Oh my God, really? Damn. You must have nerves of steel."

"Something like that." *Not anymore.*

"Wow. All this time, I've lived next door to a hero."

I think of the hard eyes I see in my reflection every morning. "I'm nobody's hero."

"Please. You're making me food. That alone would guarantee you for a cape fitting in my world. But you save the city, too. They don't call you guys in to direct traffic."

I finish straining the pasta. "I've had to direct traffic before. It's pretty dangerous, actually. Explosives are more predictable than human drivers."

"You've obviously seen me drive then."

Dammit, I like this woman. She's stunningly gorgeous, but it's hardly the most interesting thing about her. I grunt again. I don't think she's impressed by my surliness. It doesn't seem to put her off. Maybe that's because I'm cooking for her. I suppose grumpy bastards don't usually make dinner for their neighbors.

"You said 'was' like past tense when you said you were a bomb tech. Does that have something to do with the hand brace you're wearing?"

I stop stirring the milk into the pot and look at my right hand, my jaw clenching against the memory.

"I'm sorry. You don't have to tell me."

Her stricken expression brings me back into the moment and out of the one I was trying not to fall into. "It's fine. I just don't like talking about it much."

She doesn't push me, and what might have become an uncomfortable silence seems less so now. Though she winces in her seat.

"Hillary, why don't you sit on the couch? That stool doesn't look very comfortable."

"Nothing much is comfortable these days."

"Don't be stubborn. Go sit."

"You're kind of bossy, Stryker."

I push back the thought of telling her what I really want her to do. How I really want to boss her around. How I'd like to tell her to take every inch of me in her mouth. I'm torn with dueling desires that seem like they can't coexist in my head, but they do. I want to pull her hair and fuck her, and I also want to hold her hand and hand-feed her grapes. I want to treat her like a Madonna and also see my come leaking from the corner of her lips.

This woman.

I open a cabinet. Her dishes are every color of the rainbow and thick, sturdy pieces that are heavy and well made. My own plates at home match but are one step up from disposable. I bring her a bowl, a big one, of the orange pasta and before I know what I'm doing, I settle a blanket around her legs.

"Wow, you're really good at this. Take care of many preggo ladies?"

"You're my first."

She takes a spoonful, a big one, and closes her eyes in the kind of ecstasy that I feel deep in my balls. Fuck. Look at her. If she enjoys sex as much as she enjoys her dinner, she's one responsive woman. Now I'm thinking about how much I'd like to see that look on her face when I'm pumping deep inside her.

Change the subject, man. Fast. *This woman is turning you inside out.* My pulse is pounding in my dick like a motherfucker. *She's going to be somebody's mother soon, you perv.* Let it go.

You will darken her world when what she and her baby need is the sun.

But I can look out for her. Even grumpy bastards can do that much, right?

"When are you due, Hillary?"

"Seven weeks. Seven very long weeks. But then when I think about having a baby, I realize I'm not quite ready for that and seven weeks might not be long enough."

Right. Seven weeks to prepare for a virgin birth.

Chapter Three

Hillary

MAC STRYKER IS THE hottest man I've ever seen in person and that was before he brought me food. He's a god now.

Of course, that might be the stupid hormones. That is one thing they *do* talk about in the pregnancy books. I am basically hungry, tired, and horny at all times. Even while sleeping.

Is this cheese...product...supposed to taste this good? It's basically salt and chemicals, I think. Creamy, rich, wonderful salt and chemicals. The last time someone brought me macaroni and cheese and covered me with a blanket, I was probably about eight. I think it tastes better when you don't cook it for yourself.

I suppose it would be inappropriate to thank him by crawling onto his lap and rutting against him like the sex-starved lunatic I am. I understand that I am no prize right now. And it will probably be eighteen years until I have time to date once this kid pops out, and then I'll be old and nobody will want me. I am basically never going to lose my virginity.

Well, the doctor broke my hymen to make my exams easier, but I hardly think that counts.

I moan a little around a forkful of food. Sorry, not sorry.

Mac eyes my baby bump suspiciously. "How long will you keep working?"

That's a good question. "I hope to work right up until my water breaks, but I guess we'll have to see how I do closer to term. I need to save as much money as I can so I can take time off after the baby comes. I don't want to use up my savings before he or she gets here."

"You don't know if it's a boy or girl yet? I thought everyone was into those gender reveal parties now."

My turn to cock an eyebrow at him. "Yeah, how many gender reveal parties have you been to, officer?"

"Technically, that's Detective Stryker to you. And none. But I do have a Facebook account. And Pinterest."

"Wait. You have a Pinterest account?"

"Yeah. Same reason I know how to pick a lock."

"What does picking a lock have to do with Pinterest?"

His face is so tight, like maybe the furrowed ridges in his brow are permanent. "People are basically stupid. I can get a whole lot of information from social media about perps. Where they are, who they're with, what they like. Dark Tumblr is a place I wouldn't suggest you spend much time."

For a grouch, he's kind of funny. "Noted. Anyway, to answer your gender reveal party question, I want to be surprised." Aside from Joe and the girls at work, nobody really cares what the gender of my baby is anyway. It's not like my parents are going to put a sonogram picture on their fridge.

Mac rubs the skin above his hand brace, and his lips press tighter. "Mac, are you hurting right now? You didn't injure yourself more on my account, did you?"

He blinks his surprise and then realizes where he's touching. "No, it's fine."

I don't want to pull information he doesn't want to give, but I'm so curious.

"I'm off work for a while," he says quietly. "Until the hand heals..." There's more he's not saying.

"I'm sorry."

Oh, wherever he's going in his head is a painful place. I think maybe the conversation is over when he surprises me by saying, "I missed one."

"Missed one what?"

"Explosive. It went off at my last call. I got hit with debris and fucked up my hand. If it doesn't heal, I can't defuse bombs with it anymore."

Wow. I can pour a decent cup of coffee, but this guy defuses bombs and makes pregnant women macaroni and cheese. He's got to be a shoe-in for Heaven. But his frown lines deepen, and I realize he doesn't think so. "You feel responsible. About the bomb going off."

"It was my job to find them all. Stop them before anyone got hurt." He leans against the back of the couch. "Christ. I'm supposed to be talking about this with my group, not unloading it all on you."

I curl toward him more, moving into the space that separates us. "Baristas are like bartenders. I'm good at listening."

"This isn't me. I'm not a talker." There is real pain in his eyes. It finally distracts me from my horniness and propels me right into nurturing mode. I put my hand on his cheek, the stubble scruffs my hand. I hardly know him. I shouldn't be touching him like this.

Asking him to bare his soul to me.

"Hey," I say anyway. "You shouldn't feel responsible."

"My best friend died that day. Because I missed one."

"No. Mac. No. Your best friend died because a criminal rigged up a bomb. You can't take all that on."

His breathing is shallow. "Can't I? Christ. Why am I telling you this?"

"Because we're friends now."

"Are we? I've never had a woman friend before."

"I don't think it's that different. Do you?"

The way he looks at my belly, like he suspects it's another bomb he might be responsible for, is kind of endearing and a little dorky. "I think it might be different. I think it just might be."

Mac

One month later

"TELL ME WHY WE ARE watching this show again?" Tiny fucking houses. What is the point of that?

The show goes to commercial, and my only woman friend points the remote at the TV to turn it off. "Because it's my turn to pick, and I am so tired of basketball. You're like obsessed with it. I can deal with the constant bouncing, but my God, the squeaky shoes."

I set my toolbox on the shelf and test the crib I just put together. It's good and sturdy for Little Bloomer. I'm getting better at doing shit with my left hand these days. "Basketball is a great sport."

She rolls her eyes and fidgets on the couch, so I join her and pull her legs into my lap and rub her feet while she moans, the sound of it like a steel jaw clenching my balls. She has no idea how sexy I find her little moans. Or pretty much everything she does or says.

After our first dinner together last month, I was worried that I had some kind of pregnancy fetish or something, so I took to the internet to explore the dark secrets of porn and no, God no, I am not perving on the fact that she is pregnant. Thank fuck. The internet can keep some of its dark secrets, pregnancy fetish included. It seems I'm just perving on her. I have a Hillary fetish. Everything about her turns me on.

But we're just friends, for both our sakes. And it turns out, I like being friends with a woman. Except when she won't let me watch the game.

Tiny fucking houses.

She shifts again, and I have to be careful to keep her from getting into close personal contact with my junk. I don't need her to know how she affects me. Her trust is more important to me than the state of my ever-ready dick. Hillary needs me to be strong. So, I'll be strong.

If it kills me.

"Thank you for putting the crib together. Are you going to tell me how the meeting was?"

"It was like every other meeting."

The press of her lips tells me what she won't vocalize. I wish I was one of those guys who could just talk about his shit for no other reason than it will get me back on the force faster, but I get there and close up tight. The only time I feel like the old-me is when I'm with Hillary.

Her breathing changes.

"Why are you so fidgety tonight, Hillz?"

She stares straight ahead at the television, but I don't think she's really paying attention. Since it's off and she's watching it so intently anyway. "I'm not."

Okay, then.

I reach for the remote and turn the TV back on. I'm sure there's a baking show on one of these channels. A commercial comes on for some sexy movie, and she groans and squirms some more. I turn it back off.

"What is going on with you? And don't say 'nothing.'"

"Nothing," she says at the same time I say it.

"Baby, talk to me."

She sucks in a deep breath. Shit. Baby is probably not the word you call your friends.

"If you must know, it's your cologne."

My face wrinkles up. I don't wear cologne. "Do I stink or something?"

"No. It's..." She covers her face in her hands. "Hormones. Just turn the TV back on, please."

"What's hormones? I am completely lost here."

"I'm having some problems dealing with my hormones is all. And your cologne is interfering. I don't know what it is, but it smells like sex and sin and orgasms."

The air is sucked out of my lungs, and the ground is racing up to greet me like I'm falling out of the sky. Christ. "When you say hormones, do you mean you're horny?"

"Oh my God. Can we go back to tiny houses now?"

She's horny, and she thinks I smell like orgasms. My zipper cuts into my dick. I could give her orgasms. It would be my pleasure to give her orgasms. I'd love to make her come all over my hand. My tongue. My dick.

I take a chance that I know her as well as I think I do and can get her out of embarrassment mode and into what I like to call Spitfire Mode. In my most disciplined, authoritative voice, I demand, "Answer me."

She glares, which is what I wanted. "Yes, I'm horny. Happy? It's a little easier for you when you get horny, I'm sure. You just go pick a woman and let her smell you all the way back to your bed. But when you're eight months pregnant and single, it's a little more difficult. It's just biology I'm dealing with. It's not a big deal."

"You think I just pick a woman and she follows me home?"

She waves her hands. "Well, look at you. You're all chiseled and scruffy and smell so good. Who could turn you down?"

I'm trying to hold back my laugh, but she's so damn cute when she's mad. "Hillz, have you seen me pick up a woman in all the time you've lived next door to me?"

"Well, no. But the point is you can get it when you want it, and you have regular, normal biology dictating your needs, not super-amped up hormones that take over your brain and body when you're least likely to get another person to look at you naked without running the other direction." I don't think she's noticed that I'm still rubbing her feet during her epic tirade. "I have needs, Stryker. And no way to meet them."

She has needs. My God. It's been hard enough to keep off her thinking the last thing she wants is sex. Now this beautiful goddess is telling me she needs the D. What's a guy supposed to do?

"Are you even supposed to have sex—?"

"Not another word. Can we just pretend this conversation never happened? Please? Did I tell you that my tips have doubled this week? I started wearing that apron that says 'Baby on Board' and now people are throwing money at me." She pauses and looks into my eyes, knowing she hasn't distracted me. "I'm never going to get laid."

"You got laid pretty good the last time, looks like."

She shakes her head. "I didn't. I'm probably going to die a virgin. It's all so unfair."

That's it. "I think you need to explain this to me. I'm no scientist but..."

The shade of pink on her cheeks goes angry red. "Do we have to?"

"Yeah. The whole Virgin Mary thing isn't ringing true for me." I haven't pushed her since she told me she was a virgin in the hall on our first day. As soon as I figured out she doesn't need any kind of intervention because she doesn't think she's carrying the next incarnation of Jesus or anything, anyway.

Her face screws up into the look I see most often when she can't remember why she walked into a room. Which happens more frequently every day it seems. I checked and it's a normal pregnancy symptom. As is the crying for no reason sometimes, which worried me at first. "He was drunk. Really drunk."

"Who was drunk?"

Hillary rubs her pregnant belly. "You'll think less of me."

I squeeze her feet. "Baby, just tell me."

She squeezes her eyes closed. "I was interning at an ad agency in Chicago. My boss was showing me some special interest, and I let it go to my head because I was young and stupid then." As if seven months ago, she was so much younger. "I didn't know he was married. He took me to a business conference and we were fooling around in the hotel room and he was so drunk. It was the least sexy night of my life, and he was just rutting against me but never quite made...entry. There was a lot of fumbling and then he slid the condom off and...finished...in the general area. Apparently, sometimes close matters in more than just horseshoes."

Wait. What the fuck? "You got pregnant from a guy coming *on* you but not in you," I repeat to make sure I'm following the story.

I'll be damned. She really is a pregnant virgin.

"He wasn't…in the hole. Just next to it. The chances of it happening are so rare. I have a unicorn uterus or something. If he'd left the condom on, it would have been fine. But he insisted the rubber was what was making it so he couldn't come. He was such an asshole. Anyway, I guess he decided to just jerk it over me near my vagina, and I just wanted it to be over by that point."

He came on her pussy, not in it. Fuck. I didn't really think that could happen.

"When I found out I was pregnant, he didn't believe me. Said we never had sex. Told me about his wife. And wrote me a check to leave town. So I came home. Got my college summer job back, alienated my parents, and here we are. A pregnant, horny virgin who makes coffee instead of ads for a prestigious firm. Who dropped out of college her senior year. Who is mortifying her best friend."

I heard a lot in there, but I'm stuck on the last bit. "I'm your best friend?"

"Well, I hope so. I told you more than I've told anyone else."

There's something wrong with my ribs. They're too tight and feel wobbly. Unstable. Everything could go wrong with this situation. But she has needs. What if she goes to get them served elsewhere? If I twist this enough in my head, it's my duty to protect and serve her right? That's my oath as a cop. Protect and serve. Fuck. I'm not just crossing a line, I'm barreling past it like a racehorse.

"You're not going to die a virgin."

"I'll tell the line of men outside my door."

That inflames me for a second, rage changing my vision to red. The thought of other men... *Down, boy.* "You're not going to die a virgin because I am going to fuck you."

Chapter Four

Hillary

NOT GOING TO LIE. I just choked on my breath. Mac slaps my back until I push his arm away. "What did you just say?"

"You heard me."

"I don't want a pity fuck, but thanks all the same." I keep thinking I can't humiliate myself more with this guy than I already have, but I keep finding new and wonderful ways.

"You need to pay more attention if you think I'm not attracted to you. This isn't a pity fuck. This is a *two friends are horny* fuck."

Right. He's so attracted to me. Whatever. "We can't. What if it ruins our friendship?"

"Do you have no faith in me at all?"

Now would be an awesome time to pull the quilt over my head and just die of embarrassment. "Of course I do. You're a good man. The best man. But this is a lot to ask. Too much."

His big frame shifts, reminding me of all those glorious muscles. "I'm a guy. Asking me to have sex is not even on the radar of a lot to ask."

God, he smells so good. I have to shake my head to focus. "I don't want to change us. I'm not looking for a boyfriend or a baby daddy."

"Friends with benefits. I get it."

Can we really do this? No. No way. There is no way I can let him see me naked. It's hard for me to look at myself naked. "I'm a cow right now. There's no way you'll get it up."

"We can put money down, but you'll lose. I promise."

I think back to the grouch I met in the hall a month ago. He's not exactly the kind of person who lies to make someone feel good. He's more like Dr. House than Mister Rogers. Dr. House inhabiting He-Man's body. I'm getting off track because now I'm thinking about a very strange ménage situation with He-Man and Dr. House and myself and it's *not helping* with the hormones.

There is a long pause, the space between us this invisible forcefield. Heat surrounds us like a thick, syrupy steam. Who will break through it first? I want it to be him. I want him to say or do something irrevocable so that if this doesn't work, it won't be because I misread something. "How much money are we betting?"

He swallows hard. I try not to get mesmerized by the Adam's apple and fail.

Focus, Hillz.

"I mean, if I'm making a bet with you that you won't be able to get it up for me, I should know how much money I can add to Bloomer's college fund."

His eyes blaze warm fire, and he growls before reining it back in. "Before you break into your piggy bank to pay me when you lose, you should have all the facts." He reaches down and unzips, pulling out his dick for presentation.

Oh. My. God.

He's gripping it in his huge hands, and it's this enormous stalk sticking straight up, his balls and pubic hair still nestled in the opening of his jeans. Liquid beads at the top of his cock, and my core clenches hard around the ache that I should be used to by now. I'm hearing fewer arguments in my head and feeling more zapping in my underwear.

One big hand strokes up and down, spreading the sticky wetness until the whole shaft glistens. I have to squeeze my thighs together as heat pulses between my legs and my eyes lock on his huge, hard cock. My nipples tighten unbearably into aching hard little points.

"Take your clothes off, Hillary. I can guaranfuckingtee I'll stay hard."

Not once have I ever tried to be enticing to this man. He sees me in my most comfortable clothes, in my sorriest of mood swings. And right now, he could still hang a flag, a good-sized one, from his dick because he's hard *for me*. But my body doesn't look like me anymore, and I'm so nervous. So shy all of the sudden.

But I am also salivating at the sight of his cock.

Mother Nature is *such* a bitch.

This is crazy. But it's not like we can go back from here. He's got his cock out. We either move forward or we don't, but we can't go back to five minutes ago. He stands up and rips his shirt off and throws it to the floor, raising an eyebrow for me to do the same.

I'm stunned by his chest. He's not model perfect. Not at all. The physique is flawless, but his skin declares the years of using his body to fend off things most of us never think about. I know the stories for some of the scars. The knife from the night in the alley when he was a rookie. The burns. The tattoo is from a drunken escape from reality after he and Ricky responded to a shooting at a school. Mac has got a lifetime written on his skin, and I know I do too now.

Silvery lines that show where I've grown.

God. Can I do this?

I pull off my shirt and undo the bra—the very supportive and least sexy bra ever—baring my humongous tits. Hopefully they will distract him from my humongous stomach.

"You're even prettier than I imagined."

Well, okay. That's a pretty good start.

He leans over me, bracketing me between his beefy arms and the back of the couch. "Be sure, Hillary. Be very sure this is what you want. I won't miss the target like the other guy."

My breath catches at the reminder of my first failed attempt at sex and I look away, unable to let him see that far into my head. Maybe this is a bad idea.

"Hey." He cups my jaw gently in that big hand and brings my gaze back to his smoldering one. "We don't have to do this. But if we do, I'll take care of you. I'll make sure you get what you need. Do you trust me?"

It's in his eyes that I find my own courage. He's so strong, so protective. The power ripples off him and surrounds me and I know I can just let go. Let him take control. Since I met him, he's allowed me precious pockets of time where I don't have to always be on guard and responsible. He's the best friend I've ever had. "I trust you."

"I'm going to make this so good for you."

He steals my breath with a searing kiss. Surprise and delight bubble up in my throat and come out in a needy whimper as I arch toward him. His lips brand me, hot and possessive, as they slide against mine insistently. His hands move down my body, tracing liquid fire under my skin, and he turns us so my back is against the armrest and he's on top of me. He's careful, maneuvering around my bump effortlessly, but when he glides against my chest and we're skin to skin, he growls, sliding his tongue against the seam of my mouth until I open to him.

The kiss is unlike anything I've ever known before, transporting me to a new world. It's like waking up in Oz. My body comes alive, every nerve ending zapping, every inch of me trying to get closer to him. He's hot and hard everywhere, crushing against me, yet protective like he cherishes me as much as he wants to ravish me. I'm trapped in the cage of his body, yet I've never felt more free. He feeds me his tongue, and I draw him in as much as I can, my heart pounding restlessly as my blood rushes hot under my skin. He's demanding my total surrender to him, and he has it. I want him to take every part of me. I want to take every part of him. His lips move down my jaw, my neck, and when his hot, wet mouth opens on my breast, my nails score his back.

"Your fucking tits," he groans into my cleavage.

Yeah, my fucking tits are sensitive and ready for more. But they are not perky like they used to be. Heavier now. A flare of self-consciousness makes the backs of my eyes prickle. I so want to be exactly what he wants and needs. I don't want to be some kind of consolation.

"You aren't too sensitive here, are you?" He tongues my nipple, and I shake my head.

"No. It feels good. What you're doing."

"That's good news because I've been dreaming about these tits for a while."

"You have?" Was that needy sounding? I don't want to sound too needy.

"Baby, you're gorgeous."

"They're big. Even my nipples are too big..."

"You're kidding me, right? They're perfect. Your body is lush and womanly, and I've fucking jacked off a thousand times while wishing I knew the exact shade these nipples were. You're better than any fantasy I promise."

I lean back and let my eyes drift closed while he sucks greedily at me. My pulse is beating deep in my pussy, and I'm wetter than I've ever been. My body jerks unexpectedly, and I wheeze in a breath. "Oh God." He doesn't stop, thankfully understanding that the crisis I'm having is almost an orgasm. "Oh God." Just a little more. Just a little...

The cliff is sudden, and the fall fast and sharp. I lose myself and can't stop the tremors of my limbs or the husky moans that fill the air.

"Hillary, damn. You're so pretty when you come."

He strokes me gently as I come back to earth, back to the body that feels so good, so relaxed. I don't know why an orgasm with him is so different from the ones I give myself, but I'm pretty sure I'm glowing. I blink at him like I'm seeing him for the first time.

"Jesus. I'm not too far behind you." His cock is still half out of his pants and the hard length of him rubs against my leg.

"Maybe we should take the edge off yours, too."

"You worried I'm going to leave you hanging like the last guy?"

"You've already taken care of me."

"Baby, that's just an appetizer. I promise you."

He stands up, rising slowly and with such masculine grace, I start aching again. He's staring at me, and I resist the urge to cover up. He hooks his hands into the waistband of his jeans and pauses. "Are you still sure about this?"

"I'mabsolutelysure," I ramble, hoping he isn't about to take that straining package in his pants away from me.

He chuckles and lowers his pants and boxers all the way down, revealing himself to me entirely as his big cock springs up, finally free. I gasp. It's enormous, so swollen and thick. "This is how hard you make me. Do you like it?"

"Yes," I whisper. "Oh God, I want it so bad."

A rumble shakes out of his chest. "I'm going to give you every inch of it tonight. More than once, but I think you were right about taking the edge off first. You want to help me with that?"

Is he kidding me with this? My whole world just became that giant dick. "I will do absolutely anything you want, Mac. Tell me and it's yours."

He freezes, his jaw constricting and his whole body tightens. "Fuck, you don't even know what you're doing to me with that kind of talk."

"I have a pretty good idea. And that's what I want." I raise up on my elbows, licking my lips at that giant dick. "I'm going to be real with you, the way I always have been, even when it's TMI. Mac Stryker, I want you to make me your plaything. I'm so horny. I want to know what everything feels like. All of it. Teach me everything. How you taste—"

He crashes over me and kisses me fiercely. "I'm going to come all over myself if you keep talking like that." He buries his face in my neck. "Don't stop."

I feel so light when the laugh bubbles out of me. "Please do wicked, dirty things to me."

He raises his head up, looking me right in the eye. "How dirty, angel?"

"I..." Shit.

"What's wrong?"

Everything in my body tightens, and I lose focus.

"What's wrong, Hillary? Is it the baby?

I pant a few times, and then my mind clears again. "Braxton-Hicks. That one was a doozy though. I'm so sorry."

"How long have you been having them?"

"Off and on all day."

"All day?" He flies off the couch and starts getting dressed.

"It's too early for labor. It's fine, Mac. I'm just mortally embarrassed—fuck!" The pain seizes me, squeezing me from the inside out.

"We're going to the hospital."

He helps me sit up and hands me my shirt. I want to argue, but then someone jabs my spine with a lightning bolt. And my water breaks. And fuck, I'm still a virgin.

Mac

I PUT ON COP FACE BECAUSE if I don't, I will dissolve into a panic that will not be useful to Hillary or the baby currently on its way out.

These are not Braxton-Hicks contractions. I trust my gut when my gut says trouble, and we are in serious shit right now. Yes, I read the fuck out of every pregnancy book I could find, and I trained on emergency delivery, but this is scarier than a fucking bomb for damn sure. It shouldn't be happening this fast. All my spidey senses are overloading my network of logical thought processes.

Get it together, Stryker.

I dial 911. The rest starts blurring moment to moment, like I'm swimming underwater but somehow managing all the right things. Baby's not waiting. Better make a birthing nest. I tear the shower curtain down and cover Hillary's bed, piling blankets on top. I don't think I even have time to boil water.

"C'mon, sweet girl. Let's get you on the bed."

"I have a bag packed for the hospital. Maybe we can get a cab and stop for a ginger ale? For some reason, I really want a ginger ale."

Great, she's in denial.

"Let's just stay here for now and wait. The ambulance is on the way. I'll get you a ginger ale from the hospital cafeteria." I put my arms around her shoulders and lead her into the bedroom.

"I'm so sorry I didn't finish the job. Once again."

The job? Oh shit, I think she's talking about sex. It's the last thing on my mind. "All I care about right now is you and Bloomer."

I leave the apartment door open for the paramedics, and get Hillary settled on the bed when she starts to panic. A little late, but not unexpected. "Wait. No. I can't do this now. Here. We have to go. I can't have my *baby* in this apartment."

"We don't have time to go, honey. All you need to worry about right now is breathing. I'll do the rest."

"No. No. No." She screws up her face in pain. "No! Not now. Why is this happening so fast? I'm supposed to be at the hospital."

I don't know why this is happening so fast, but something isn't right. I'm scared as fuck. The last time someone's life depended on me, I let him down.

I know better than to go there now. I push thoughts of the last call out of my head and focus. Hillary needs me. Her baby needs me. Whatever is going on isn't going to pause so I can have a mental breakdown. I have to focus.

When the paramedics come in the door, Little Bloomer is already crowning. One uniform tries to take my place, but I shake my head, my focus solely on the baby. I don't trust anyone else. It's too important. The woman crouches on the floor next to me and the other EMT supports Hillary's back.

"She should push now," the woman next to me says.

I nod. Hillary is too pale. "I need you to push, angel. Can you do that?"

"I'm scared, Mac."

I lock eyes with her. "You're doing great. You're going to be such a great mom. I promise. I'm right here."

"You make everything easier, Mac."

She fucking detonates my heart.

And then she screams, and the pushing begins. In between pushes, Hillary won't look at anything but me. I want to take all this pain into myself, free her of it. I couldn't stand it when she cried about her ankles, so this screaming in pain is killing me.

"Get it out of me, Mac!"

"We're working on it, angel. Let's do the breathing again."

"Fuck you."

The EMTs know better than to laugh, but I have a hard time keeping it in. I guess if she's swearing at me, she's still herself. She screams again, giving it her all, and I catch Little Bloomer sliding out.

Holy fuck. I just caught a baby.

The baby looks at me with these eyes too wise for someone brand new into this world, my heart explodes again.

Words. There should be words for what I'm feeling. The way the whole planet just started turning the other way. I don't have words. I choke on what might be tears balling up in my throat.

"It's a girl, Hillary."

"Is she okay?"

"She's perfect."

We clean up the baby and put her onto Hillary's chest. We still need to get to the hospital, and that's a process with the stairs and the stretcher and the ambulance. I ride near her head and she looks up at me. "I want to call her Kenzie. MacKenzie Bloom. Kenzie."

I kiss her temple and the adrenaline rush I've been on starts to dissolve, leaving me shaky. Kenzie. "I like that," I choke out, hoping my voice just sounds manly and not obvious that I'm trying not to cry.

"Thank you for bringing her here safely, Mac."

"You did all the hard work, babe."

She smiles and closes her eyes for a little hard-earned rest.

The machine screams, and I look on the floor for a loose cord. We must have hit a bump. The EMT thrusts the baby at me. "Sir, you need to scoot back. You

THE HELL WITH THE WORLD spinning the opposite way. Now it's upside down.

Hillary won't wake up.

She came out of emergency surgery three hours ago. I've been pacing the halls since we got here. I can't fix this. I can't show up in my gear and defuse anything. I can't take down a bad guy. Nothing I know how to do applies now.

I don't know how to be a man who paces a hall.

"Detective Stryker?"

I turn, my heart stops while I wait for the nurse in scrubs to fill me in about Hillary. "Your daughter is ready for a feeding. Would you like to feed her?"

"I—"

Compassion and patience soften the nurse's face. "There's nothing you can do for your wife but wait. Your daughter can benefit from bonding with her daddy, though. And I think your wife would want you to take care of her while she can't."

My wife. My daughter. Daddy.

The paramedics just assumed we were married. It didn't occur to me to correct them while they were trying to stabilize Hillary's heart. Then, it made things easier in the hospital. I'll probably get in trouble for lying, but nobody would have kept "the neighbor" in the loop about Hillary's surgery. So, I'm now a husband and father.

Pacing isn't helping, and the nurse is right. "Yeah, okay. I'll feed Kenzie." I take two steps then stop. "I don't know how."

"I'll help you." She brings me to a nursery and sets me up in a rocking chair before she hands me the baby swaddled up tight in a pink blanket.

"Is her blanket too tight?"

"Most babies love it. It's reassuring to them. They're used to not having much room."

That makes sense.

The nurse shows me how to hold the bottle and promises to come back to show me how to burp the baby when she's through. As long as her neck is supported, I guess I'm doing all right. The nurse walks away and leaves me almost alone with a baby for the first time ever. Am I supposed to talk to her? Sing? I don't know what is going on.

Kenzie seems to have a better handle on things. She's drinking from the bottle and watching me. I read everything about pregnancy I could find in the last month. It never occurred to me to read about how to take care of a baby once it's born. I guess I assumed I wouldn't have much to do with that.

"Hey, Kenzie. Um, your mom is sleeping. When she wakes up, she's really going to want to meet you, though." Kenzie blinks. "You're really going to like your mom. She's great. So funny. And she's good at taking care of stuff. You won't believe all the houseplants in your apartment. She talks to them. Well, you've heard her." I swallow around that damn ball in my throat. I'm *not* a dude who cries. "We haven't really met. I mean, I was the guy that caught you—nice form by the way, you nailed the dismount. I help your mom sometimes. I bet you've heard my voice, right? I've been hanging out a lot lately. Your mom and I are friends. Don't tell anyone that though, okay? While we're here, we have to pretend I'm your dad. I'll explain later.'

Her little eyelids get heavy. Either I'm boring as shit, or she likes the sound of my voice.

"So, the thing is, if you need anything, you're going to always just tell me. Okay? I mean, when you can talk. Until then, I'll just have to guess. But when you're older, if you have questions about stuff or want to learn how to make a three-point shot, you just call me."

The nurse comes back and shows me the proper burping procedure. Kenzie lets a good one go. "Just like your mom," I tell her and the nurse laughs. She leaves us again, and I just rock, not sure what else to do. Kenzie sniffles as she's falling asleep. I'll remember this moment forever. The sound of her tiny breaths, the sweet smell of her head, the slight weight of her resting on my chest.

I feel a kind of peace I'm not used to, and in that peace, the thoughts I've been keeping out of my head finally break through. What happens if Hillary doesn't wake up?

She has to. She just has to. Now that my heart has inflated to full size, it would kill me if it shattered. I can't lose her. I certainly can't pretend to be Kenzie's dad, but fuck anyone who tries to put her in foster care. And fuck the asshole who wrote a check to keep this tiny baby out of his life. She's a fucking miracle.

Please, don't let her lose her mom before she gets her.

Chapter Five

Hillary

THE BEEPING. WON'T somebody stop the beeping?

I try to reach for my phone even though I don't think it's my alarm. I can't quite get my arm to move or my brain to think. Am I napping? What is even...?

"Relax, Hillary."

I try to open my eyes, but it takes a lot of effort. "Mac?"

I don't think my voice worked when I said that, nothing seemed to come out, but he starts talking again. "Relax. You're fine. The baby is fine. You're in the hospital. You had surgery, so you need to take it easy. Don't try to talk. I'll get a nurse, and we can get you a drink of water."

The baby?

Bits and pieces start occurring to me. The labor, the ambulance ride. Then...it all feels too much, too overwhelming. I want to say that I want to see the baby, but I feel the fog of sleep coming back. I fight it. But it's easier to sink back down than swim against the current.

When I blink my eyes open again, the light in the room has changed. I must have slept awhile. Mac is sleeping in the chair next to my bed. On his chest, also sleeping, is the most beautiful baby I've ever seen. Her little nose, oh my God. Nobody told me her little nose would be so perfect.

I hear another noise and turn my head toward a nurse fiddling with the bag attached to me. "You're awake." She smiles. "Your husband is going to be so happy. He hasn't left this hospital in two days."

My husband?

Maybe I woke up in an alternate reality. It wouldn't be so bad. To be married to Mac. Be a real family.

My thoughts begin to unjumble as I take in more of my surroundings. I hear a muted television laugh track nearby, maybe the room next door. My mouth is dry and tastes like I've been chewing on chalk. There's a soft drip near me, probably the bag of fluids I'm hooked up to. The nurse's fingers are cold as she counts my pulse. She helps me sit up some, and Mac comes fully awake.

"Hey," I say. He looks so tired and so beautiful. His new growth beard is dark. It's a good look for him. The red eyes don't even take away from how handsome he is.

"Hey yourself."

The nurse tsks. "I'm going to see if the doctor is still doing rounds. I know he'd like to see you. An ice chip or two only until I get orders for clear liquids."

Mac brings Kenzie closer so I can touch her. Smell her. "Thank you for being here. The nurse said you've been here the whole time?"

"Where else would I be?"

"She called you my husband."

He grins. The Grinch is grinning. "Yeah. About that—"

"Congratulations." We both look at the door where a well-dressed woman about ten years older than I am is holding a bouquet of balloons that look garishly cheerful next to her icy expression. Surely she's not a hospital volunteer. She enters the room, setting the balloons on a chair that mauve color that dominated the '80s. "My name is Melinda Foster. I believe you are acquainted with my husband."

"I don't—" Then I remember Ashton Foster, my boss in Chicago. "Oh."

"Yes, oh." She peers at the baby like she's a bauble in the window at Tiffany's. "The baby is very pretty."

Mac is quiet, but his presence is loud. Stable. Is she going to confront me here? Now? Why would she bring balloons? How did she even—

"I'm sure you have questions, so I'll just get right to the point. While I'm not happy my husband chooses to seduce his interns every year, he was a bit hasty in sending you away. You see, I can't have children."

"I'm very sorry." I don't know what else to say. I am sorry she can't have kids. I'm sorry that I almost had sex with her husband before I knew he was married.

"I know he paid you. That's how I found out about you. I'm offering to pay you more."

"Look, I'm not coming after him if that's what you're worried about."

"You misunderstand, Miss Bloom. I'm offering to double what he paid you. I want the baby."

Mac

"EXCUSE ME?" HILLARY winces when she tries to sit up too fast.

"We can give your daughter the kind of life you can't. Think about it, Hillary. She'll never want for anything. What can you give her? How are you even going to be able to afford her? I know he didn't give you much. Certainly most of it will go to your hospital bill now."

She's ice-cold. All that's missing is a shock of white hair and a coat made from Dalmatians. "I think you better go, Mrs. Foster."

Hillary hasn't said anything, but she's blending in with her bedsheets in a bad way.

The puppy stealer turns her icy eyes to me. "And who are you?"

"Our daughter is not for sale. You need to go before I call security."

"Your daughter." She huffs. "Well played, Hillary. So you snagged yourself a good-looking man to trick into fatherhood. Just think, now you can let him off the hook. Unless of course, you want to keep him. In which case, I probably threw a wrench in your little plan. So sorry."

She's anything but sorry. "If you continue to harass my family, I will make sure you are very, very sorry indeed."

Her face cracks. "Who are you exactly?"

"Well. I'm a cop, exactly. One who can arrest you for about four things since you got to town, including whatever lie you told at the nurses station to get access to my wife's room. Maybe you should try to legally adopt a child instead of purchase a cop's baby."

The woman is shrewd and knows she won't get any further here. She doesn't even say goodbye, just turns and leaves.

Hillary hasn't regained her color. I take her hand. "I'm sorry she got in here. You need to rest. That wasn't good for your recovery."

"What if she's right?"

My stomach pitches uncomfortably. "What?"

"Kenzie could have a princess life. I might not even be good at this. Maybe she would be better off—"

"Don't finish that. She belongs with you. Nobody will ever love this little girl more than you can. Nobody."

I tuck the baby in under Hillary's arm and the tension breaks as she looks down at her baby. "Oh, she's so lovely."

I grab a tissue and dab her eyes. "She takes after her momma."

"So what is going on with this getting married bit? How long was I sleeping, exactly?"

"The hospital thinks we're married, and I didn't correct them so I could stay with you. I've just been taking things on the fly as we go."

"On the fly, huh? Something you learned how to do from your 'perps,' I bet."

"Just thinking on my feet." I pull the chair up. "There's something else you should know. I'm listed on Kenzie's birth certificate."

Hillary just blinks at me.

Shit.

"They brought me the form while you were still in a coma, thinking we were married. I was afraid what would happen to Kenzie if you... didn't wake up. I shouldn't have put my name on it without talking to you, but you weren't answering me. So, I made sure Kenzie was taken care of."

What happened to my oath of not getting close to anyone? I'm now on the hot seat with Hillary, and the legal father of a newborn.

"I didn't think you could top the macaroni and cheese dinner, but you really are a hero, aren't you?"

Breath expels from my lungs in a rush. "I lied. To a lot of people. I'm not sure that makes me a hero."

Hillary reaches out for my hand. "You took care of my baby when I couldn't. I don't think I can ever repay you for making sure she wouldn't be alone, with nobody fighting for her."

I knew in my head I was going too far, but in my heart if felt like the right thing to do. And my heart is totally fucked up right now. "Just get better, Hillary. That's how you can repay me."

Chapter Six

Hillary

Two months later

TODAY HAS BEEN A GOOD day. I know better than to expect to feel like this very often, but I got six hours of uninterrupted sleep last night plus a nap this afternoon. I kind of feel like a new person. I just finished a feeding, and Mac is rocking Kenzie to sleep. Well, she's already asleep. He's just rocking her. She's a little pink lump on his massive chest, so small in his big man hands. The sound of his heartbeat always soothes her so much. She must know she's safe. Nothing can hurt her when she's in his gentle hands.

What's not safe is my libido. Holy fuckballs. A beefy alpha man with a teeny tiny baby on his chest would put a little spring in any woman's ovaries. The fact that it's *my* teeny tiny baby adds a triple Axel to that spring. "You going to put that baby to bed soon?"

He grunts. "I like her when she's sleeping."

"You don't fool me. You like that baby all the time. So much for being my grouchy neighbor."

He gets out of the chair with this masculine grace that makes me jealous. Especially since he does it without waking the baby. Something I haven't mastered yet. "We should take her to the park tomorrow."

"She's a little young for the slide."

"I was thinking more about fresh air. And that maybe you could use some too."

It's been a few days since I left the apartment. Two? Three? "Yeah, you know, that might be a good idea." Since I can't remember what outside feels like.

He tucks Kenzie into her crib and winces when he straightens.

"What's wrong? You hurt yourself at the gym?"

He rubs his shoulder. "I pushed too hard today. My traps and lats," he says like that's something I would understand.

"That means…"

"That means I should get you down to the gym. Then you'd know."

"Ha. Not happening. Unless that's your way of insinuating I'm out of shape." More like he's just kind of bossy about what he thinks is good for me. Which I allow because it's nice to be cared for.

Mac gets down two glasses and pours the non-alcoholic wine for us. "I wouldn't mind if you were stronger just because I want you to be able to defend yourself."

"You're just tired of opening all my jars."

"I'll always open jars for you."

We sort of pause there, like our conversation is on DVR. There is this long exchange where the two of us just stare into each other's eyes. In a moment that should have been uncomfortable or strange, instead there is a connection. I don't want to read too much into what he said, but "always" is a long time, and I'm having a hard time with remembering we're *just friends* lately. He's with us a lot. He takes care of Kenzie like a dad. He even spent the night in my bed last week when she was getting up every twenty minutes. A very platonic night in my bed, but still.

He's in boyfriend mode except for the part where there is any kind of affection that isn't platonic.

We still haven't addressed what we were doing on the couch when I went into labor. It was stricken from the record, I guess. And for a while, it needed to be. But my girl parts are defrosting again after their hiatus, and my hot neighbor fantasies are warming up.

I need to break this weird silence, though. "So, what is a…what did you call it that's sore? Trats?"

He hands me a glass. "Lats and traps. Turn around."

I take a sip and turn as he places a large, strong, warm hand on my upper back.

"Here and…" He slides his hand onto my shoulder. "Here."

My heart sprints from his touch, giving me a good workout after all. My breath grows heavy. "Oh." I wish this wine had real booze right now. I could use the liquid courage. No drinking until I'm done nursing, though.

"Wow, you're pretty tense, too." His hand gently kneads my shoulder.

He's touched me plenty in the last three months. I'm not sure what is different right now. Why his hot breath on my skin causes my nipples to pucker under my shirt. Why, when I let myself go lax against his hard body behind me, I have to hold in the moan.

"You're all knotted up. Your shoulders are stiffer than mine."

Why don't you show me how stiff you are?

Down, girl.

I groan when he works out one of those knots with his thick hands. "I think my knots have knots. This isn't hurting your right hand, is it? You just stopped wearing the brace."

"Don't worry about my hand. Just relax."

I loll my head to one side and release all the tension in my body. Mac's breathing becomes louder, and his dick presses against my ass but neither of us comment on it. Is he taking as much pleasure from massaging me as I am from his magic hands? "It feels really good, Stryker." I take a chance and press my ass against his hardening dick.

He doesn't say a word as he slowly slides one of his hands down my side to the waistband of my shorts and tugs lightly at my nursing top, exposing a patch of skin to his tracing fingers.

We've gone too far to call this an innocent massage now. I guess it's time to do the big girl thing and make a move. A real one.

I reach behind me and rub his erection. "Feels like you're stiff, too, Stryker. I think you need a rubdown as much as I do."

Mac

I GROAN AND REST MY chin on her shoulder, inhaling the soft skin of her neck. Fuck, I want her... I want Hillary so badly. I've spent countless nights either jacking myself to sleep thinking about her or dreaming of her in ways I felt guilty about in the morning. I want to see her naked little body, put my hands on the breasts that are incredibly generous for her frame, hold her hips as I discover how tight and hot she is...

But this isn't right. She's just had a baby and surgery. I have nothing to offer her. I'm still not cleared to go back to work. I still can't talk about the last call I went on and what happened to Ricky. I still wake up in a cold sweat most nights. I feel like half the man I used to be, and that guy was no prize either. Not good enough for her or Kenzie. "Hillary..."

"Shhhh," she says, "you don't have to say anything." She turns so she's facing me and sets her NA wine on the counter. The pulse in her throat is leaping as she runs her hands from my wrists up to my shoulders and then curls them around the back of my neck. She stands on tiptoe and gently lays her lips on mine. She pulls back and tenderly traces my lower lip with the pad of her thumb.

Fuck if I know what to do with this sweetness. I clutch her arms, my limbs shaky and weak. "I'm not sure this—"

Hillary pulls my head down to rest my forehead against hers with a sigh. Cupping both my cheeks, she softly uses her fingertips to comb through my hair. Stretching up to me again, just a breath away from my lips, she whispers, "I'm sure." She leans forward just enough to barely touch her lips to mine. Then she whispers again, "I'm very, very sure." With a smile, she pulls me closer to meet her lips fully. Her mouth slides over mine, lips clinging, sipping.

Her mouth curves in pleasure when I return her kiss. I don't rush this, though part of me wants to. It's just a soft, gentle exploration, like we have all the time in the world. I tell myself we'll stop soon. Take it slow. There's this feeling inside me that keeps fluttering just out of my grasp, and I know if I try to hold it, it will disappear. I need to just let this sweetness happen.

I part my lips in invitation, not wanting to push. But it's getting harder. *I'm* getting harder. Softly, she touches the inside of my mouth, tasting and exploring me, like she's learning my flavor as she slides her tongue against mine.

Time spins out, and I lose myself in her. My hands are in her hair, her body flush against mine. All that softness and warmth that I don't deserve, yet I take. And take.

Her hands are under my shirt, stroking my chest and torso, creating little patterns of sparks wherever her fingertips land. I try to reach for her wrists. "Wait."

"Done waiting." Her hands are pulling up the hem of my shirt, and any war I might have been fighting is over when I see the sheer delight in her eyes as she uncovers me. Fuck, her desire undoes me. I rip the shirt off and tug her to me, delving back into her luscious lips. It's not sweet kisses anymore. I'm all-out assaulting her mouth, fucking her with my tongue, bringing as much of her body against me as I can and holding her tightly. Maybe too tightly. Months of stored sexual tension just broke the dam of careful control I'd cultivated, and I can't give a fuck.

I pick her up, mauling her on the way to her bedroom. Her legs wrap around my waist and she grinds on my cock. Damn, that's good.

I set her on her feet next to the bed and I try to find thoughts through the haze of lust. "Wait. Are you okay to do this? Is it too soon?"

"Doctor cleared me at my last appointment. I didn't say anything because, well, we weren't...we haven't been..."

"And we are now?"

"We are now for sure." She bites her lip and looks at the tent in my shorts. "I need you, Mac."

Rockets burst in my damned ribcage. Want can't begin to describe what I'm feeling. "Baby, there's two men warring inside me right now. One wants to make love to you slow and sweet and treat you like a princess."

"And the other?"

Dare I? Will I scare her off? Maybe that's best. If she sees the ugly parts, maybe she'll protect herself.

I wind her hair around my hand and tug, exposing her throat to me. I close my mouth over her skin and nip, then lave it with my tongue. "The other wants to fuck you dirty and raw and treat you like a toy."

Chapter Seven

Hillary

A RUSH OF MOISTURE dampens my panties. "Okay, yes. Both. Please."

He looks at me carefully, like he's not sure I'm really here. "I don't want to scare you."

"I kind of want to be scared. Don't hold back with me, okay? Promise?"

He makes a low sound in the back of his throat. "I'm not sure I can hold back."

"Then don't." I lower to my knees.

"Hillary—"

Using both my hands, I pull his shorts and underwear down slowly, cherishing the reveal of his giant, fat cock. I've dreamed about getting this close to it ever since that afternoon two months ago. Hell, probably longer than that. But that was when I got to see if for the first time. That's when I knew I wanted to see it again.

It springs up, protruding from his body and resting mere inches from my face. A small, clear bead of pre-cum tops its slit. I lick my lips, and the fluid begins to trickle out more. I take his cock in both my hands because one hand won't be able to fully close around the throbbing girth of him.

I had a little bit of false bravado going on the last few minutes, but it's been replaced by feelings much stronger. Suddenly, every dirty story, every porno, every naughty desire is flashing in front of my brain. I'm discovering that I have an inner slut, she's a bit cock-hungry, and I like her. I have a feeling Mac is going to like her too.

"I need to be used as much as I need to use you, Mac." I stick my tongue out and lick the clear beads running down the underside of its swollen crown. His desire for me is delicious.

"Oh fuck. You don't have to do this. Oh fuck."

I circle the tip with my tongue. "I really want to, Mac."

"Christ, that feels good." He looks down at me and brushes the hair from my face. There's so much going on in his gaze.

He's spent the last three months respecting me, being my friend, my partner. But there's a primal side he's been keeping from me. I think if I can get him to let it out, it won't wreck us like he thinks it will. I think it will make us stronger. I rub his dick on my face. Lovingly. Wantonly. I *need* it. I *crave* it.

"Hillary, are you sure?"

"Yep." I pop just the tip of him in and out of my mouth quickly, like punctuation on my answer. "But Mac..." I remember that day on my couch. How hot he was for me. How much he liked it when I said I wanted him to do everything to me. Show me everything. Make me his plaything. I want him back there, in that headspace. I use his dick like lip balm, running it around my lips and then I lick my lips slowly, making sure he sees my enjoyment of him. "I've never done this before. Remember? I need you to teach me. I want to learn *everything*."

He moans, clutching my face in one hand. He reaches down and takes my hand and wraps it firmly around his cock. It is hot and thick and hard and velvety smooth. With his hand around mine, he begins to stroke, teaching me a rhythm. "That's it, baby. Just like that. So good." After a few minutes, he leans forward and presses the tip of his dick to my lips. "In your mouth," he demands, his voice deep and husky.

Oh fuck. I like it when he tells me what to do. He slides his fat cock into my mouth, the sensation overwhelming and intoxicating.

"Open your eyes," he says. This command, made with authority, makes me shiver. "Look at me. Look into my eyes."

The air shifts around us like we're traveling someplace we can only go together. "That's it. Keep looking at me. I want all your attention. You watch who's fucking your mouth."

I'm in some kind of trance. A cock trance, I guess. I never thought I would feel this connected. The eye contact with his cock in my mouth is almost too much. I want to retreat but know I can't.

"Oh fuck," he says with a hiss. "That sweet little mouth of yours...I want to fill it up." He holds my head still as I swirl my tongue all over the hot surface of his crown. As he starts to roll his hips in slow circles, I let my lips follow the silky-smooth surface of his shaft as he forces more of it into my mouth.

His erection is rock hard, yet the surface feels velvety smooth against my lips. How can something be so hard and yet so soft at the same time? He moves his hands lovingly through my hair, directing me along his cock. It seems to grow a little bit harder and bigger as it throbs. I know he's close. My own body is tingling all over.

"Yeah, baby, just like that...suck my cock the way I like it."

The words ricochet around my head. I want every filthy naughty word he knows.

"Look at you with those pretty eyes looking at me while I fuck your mouth. What a good girl you are. You love my cock, don't you?"

"Mmmm." The vibrations of my moan makes him tighten his hold on my head. The sheer size of his cock wildly turns me on, but it's the way he's starting to allow himself to let go with me that makes my pussy pulse with need. He slowly bucks his hips back and forth then starts full-on thrusts, pumping his cock in and out of my mouth, stretching my lips tightly around his massive member.

"Oh God. Baby, you feel so good. I don't want to come yet, but you're going to make me, aren't you? Naughty girl. So greedy. Are you ready for it? Are you going to swallow my come, sweet thing?"

I nod. I want it. I feel like some kind of junkie. I've fooled around with a few guys, but never swallowed. Never wanted to. But I want to know what it will feel like when I take him all the way, when his essence slides down my throat. God. I'm loving feeling so slutty.

"Oh fuck, Hillary...Fuck... here it comes!" he groans. Mac grunts loudly over and over, and the underside of his cock pulses against my tongue as it pumps jets of come. My mouth fills with him, and I have to swallow repeatedly to keep it from spilling out. I begin to think he'll never stop coming. I just keep swallowing. When he finally finishes, his dick starts to soften, and I lick it all over and let it fall from my mouth.

He's breathing hard, his chest heaving up and down, and his cock lays heavily against his thigh. Wet and glistening.

"Oh, Jesus," he pants. "Baby, that was amazing. I've never come that hard. Or that much. Are you okay?"

My chest fills with feminine pride. "I feel fantastic."

"You just fucking wait."

Mac

I TUG HER HAND, PULLING her up and wrench her shorts down to her ankles. "You've been a very good girl, making me come so hard. It's time for your reward." I push her onto the bed and kneel between her legs. My thick finger looks obscenely big on her pussy as I part her puffy, wet lips. I slide my finger slowly up the smooth inside of her wet skin.

Beautiful.

She's pretty worked up from giving me that incredible blow job, her body wracking with tremors if I even skim lightly over her clit. "Oh, you like that, do you? You like me touching your pretty pussy? You're so wet, sweetheart. You must have really liked having my cock in your mouth." I rub her clit with slow, tight, small circles and use a little pressure as I move my other hand between her legs and slide two fingers into her. She bucks against my large fingers, moving herself up and down on them, as her juices ran down my hand. My other hand works the pearl of her clit in circles, slowly increasing pressure. "Look at you, fucking yourself on my fingers. You're making me get hard again already."

She moans loudly and continues to thrust herself up and down on my fingers. She grabs my wrist, sending my fingers deeper into her. I stop and bring my hand to my mouth as she cries at my sudden exit.

"Watch me lick you off my fingers, sweetheart." Her eyes dilate as I savor the taste of her. "So fucking good."

I quickly bring her up into a sitting position and pull her top off over her head. Those fucking tits. I've been teased with glimpses of them every time she nurses Kenzie. Her nipples are puffier now than before she gave birth. Wider like silver dollars. The shape of her is so womanly, so lush.

She covers her scar from surgery, but I pull her hand away and kiss it. "You don't get to hide anything from me now."

She lays back down, and I move on top of her, and we grind together and kiss like horny teenagers. Slowly, I start to kiss down her throat, nuzzling the space between her neck and her shoulders and down toward the slopes of her beasts. She tangles her hands in my hair and urges me to move lower, so I kiss down her body, savoring her succulent curves. Lower and lower, inhaling deeply as I veer to her thighs. With each kiss she moans as I get closer and closer to her pussy.

"Please."

"Please, what, sweetheart?" I nip at her skin.

"Stop teasing me. I need to come," she groans, her fingers digging into my scalp.

Laughing, I lower my mouth to her pussy, slowly licking, committing her taste to my memory. Salty, musky, slightly sweet.

Her hips are grinding and thrusting up toward me now, her breath getting shorter and shorter. "I could eat you all night." I concentrate my lips and tongue on her hard little clit, sucking it into my mouth and flicking it with my tongue as I finger her pussy, curling my finger toward her G-spot.

She moans and her pussy contracts around my finger, her body convulsing off the bed. "That's it, angel. Come all over my hand. Such a good girl."

Watching each flash of pleasure spark through her body and onto her face as she hurtles through her orgasm makes me feel like a goddamn king. Her ecstasy is my reward. I want more.

I get a condom, wishing I didn't have to. As I put it on, I look at her shapely body spread out below me. Glowing and dazed from the orgasm I gave her. I want to feel her come around my dick. "Do you know how many times I've imagined taking you? How I've stroked my hard cock thinking about pushing into your tight little wet cunt?" I reach down to grip the outsides of her thighs, positioning myself between them. I grab my cock and rub it between her drenched pussy lips. "Are you sure about this, sweetheart?" I ask, rubbing her slit with the tip of my aching cock, praying to God she hasn't changed her mind.

"I'm sure, Mac. I'm so sure. Do it. Fuck me."

I growl, pausing with the head barely inside her. "Look at me," I whisper harshly, grasping her chin and forcing her gaze on me again. "I want to see the look in your eyes when I enter you."

I push in slow, achingly slow, but I don't want to hurt her and damn, she feels so good. Something happens in our eye contact. Something raw and more intimate than I've ever felt before. She tenses, just as taken aback by it as I am. Something pushes at my chest from the inside, an ache heavy and wanting. I push in and her body goes rigid.

"Relax, sweetheart. Don't clench up." She exhales like she's forgotten she hadn't, and I ease all the way into her tight channel. I begin pushing in and out of her in slow, controlled, shallow thrusts. "You feel so perfect around me."

I pull her legs higher around my waist in an attempt to penetrate her deeper. My cock is a steel rod, throbbing with anticipation, but I pause long enough to feel how hot and tight she encases me. Her slick walls welcome me, heating up my shaft.

"Mmm," Hillary moans as my cock fills her snug pussy, and I push against her mound.

"Am I too hard for you, sweetheart? Am I too big?" I ask roughly, pushing myself deeper and hoping to God she says no but still going slow.

"You feel so good," she whispers. Our eyes lock on each other again, and neither of us move as her pussy muscles compress around my cock. She grips my face in her hands and pulls me in for a kiss, digging her heels into my ass and pushing me deeper inside. We grind against each other, not even fucking exactly. Just grinding in this slow rhythm that takes me down to my core animal.

Her inner muscles tighten and pulse around me, and I know I won't be able to go slow much longer. I reach under and grab her ass as I thrust deeper into her. "Tell me."

"Tell you what?"

"Tell me you're okay. That you need it. I'm barely holding on here, sweetheart."

"I feel every inch of you inside me and I still want more. Make me yours, Mac." She rocks against my cock. "Fuck me like you own me."

Fuck. That does it. Like a starting gun has gone off in my head, I pound her pussy, pushing on her clit with my pelvic bone on each downward thrust. I can't remember ever being this hard.

She keeps moaning and calling my name. "Oh fuck! Oh Mac! Oh God!" she calls out as I slam my cock home again and again until we're both reduced to grunting animals.

She plants her feet on the mattress and arches her back as I hammer into her fiery heat. This bed is going to catch on fire. I have to slide my hands under her back and grip her shoulders to keep her from hitting the headboard.

I'm driving into her like a hammer to a nailhead. Deeper. Harder. Fuck. I'm being too rough, but it's hard to stop or slow or think when she's egging me on. I reach between us and get a thumb on her engorged clit. "Come, baby. Come all over my cock. I want to feel you milking my dick."

Hillary screams, thrashing her head from side to side and digging her fingers into my back as her orgasm hits her full force. My balls tighten, and my blood goes lava hot. My cock lurches inside her, her inner muscles clamping tightly around it. White lights blur my vision as I throw my head back and roar. We ride out the pulsating waves of pleasure as I jerkily discharge my heavy load into the condom, hoping to hell it can hold it all.

Chapter Eight

Hillary

I'M A PRETTY LIGHT sleeper lately, so when I notice a change in Mac's body next to me, I wake up right away. We'd fallen asleep with me on his chest, both of us warm and languid and boneless. Now he's stiff, tight, and his heart is pounding too fast under my cheek.

I lift my head. Clock says 2:14. Kenzie will be up soon.

I wipe my mouth and chin for stray sleeping drool and consider the man I'm curled against. I need to be so careful. What he did to my body, what I did to his, brought me to another plane of existence. A girl could get used to the kind of orgasms that wring out her body.

Don't.

I know, I know.

I promised myself that I would be enough for my child when her bio-dad dumped us. When my parents were too disappointed in me to keep loving us. I can't let my heart lead us to that kind of hurt again. I have to be enough for her and for me. It's nice having Mac around, but I can't get used to it or depend on him too much. I have to make sure that if we remain friends with benefits, it stays friends with benefits. It's too easy to rely on him like he'll always be there. When your own parents break up with you, you learn nobody is really safe. Nobody stays forever.

I just have to be strong. Enjoy his body. His time. His infinite patience. His sense of honor. His humor. His heart...fuck, I'm falling for him and I can't. I absolutely cannot.

His body tenses below me again, and I realize he's dreaming. It doesn't seem like a happy one. He shoots upright, gasping, and I get bounced off him back to my own side of the bed.

I scramble back to him. "Mac, it's okay. You're dreaming. It's a bad dream."

He looks at me with a lax expression, his eyes cloudy and unfocused.

"You were having a dream," I repeat and reach for his shoulder. It's clammy, and he shrugs me off him and bolts out of bed.

"Sorry." He searches the floor for his pants, his movement erratic and jerky. "I should go. Sorry I woke you."

"No big deal. It's almost time for—" my speech is broken off by Kenzie's muffled cry on the baby monitor. "Well, you know." I laugh it off as I roll out of bed, but the laughter is forced. I feel a lot more naked right now than I did when he was inside me.

I don't like this sense of bewilderment I feel. I don't want to get too close to him, but I don't appreciate feeling like he's pulling away either. He isn't looking at me. He *won't* look at me.

I know this feeling. This sinking of the heart. I drop my chin to my chest. I've been here before. I tug on the first clothes I find, wanting not to be visible.

"I'll go—" my voice cracks, so I clear it. "I'll go feed Kenzie. You can...stay."

"No, I should..."

"Right. Okay. Well, see you tomorrow then."

I rush out of the room, past him and into the living room where Kenzie's crib is. I pull it together with a deep breath and reach in to get her. "Hello, hungry baby. Mommy's here."

As soon as she is in my arms, I feel more centered again. She's already rooting around on my shirt as I walk to the rocking chair. Hungry baby is right. Mac comes out looking more himself.

"Sorry that was weird. I...the dream. I just have trouble shaking it sometimes."

I settle Kenzie on my breast. "Sure, yeah. It's fine."

"I'm going to go home, but I'll see you later today, right? We still on for the park later?"

I nod and force a smile. He leans down and kisses the top of my head and then the top of Kenzie's head. She doesn't notice. Food is all she needs right now. And that I can give her. I have serious doubts about my ability to provide her with what she'll need as the years progress, but right now, I can do this. And I don't need anyone.

When the door latches, I let out a shuddering breath and tug the baby closer. "We'll figure it out together, baby. You and me together. Against the world."

Later that day, Mac stops by with the mail, just like most days. I should probably tell him I can get my own mail. It would be good for me to look at all the ways I've insinuated him into our lives and start taking baby steps away from them. Like that old saying goes about people coming into your life for a season or something. The fact that it hurts to think of him not being a part of my everyday life is the very reason I should start the process sooner. If he stops coming and I'm not prepared, it will hurt more.

That's when I see it.

A card in a pink envelope with my mother's writing. My belly knots.

"Why are you shaking?" Mac asks me and immediately comes to my side.

"Um. Maybe I didn't eat enough."

He looks right through me and then looks at the pile of mail. "What is upsetting you about that card?"

I blow out a slow breath. "It's from my mother."

"You don't talk much about your parents."

"There's not much to say. They wanted me to go to this old school maternity home thing and give my baby away. They didn't want their friends or the people from church to know that I had fallen." I push the card away from me. "They told me they wouldn't pay for anything unless I did it their way, so I left. Old Joe hired me back on. I sold my car since I only live a couple blocks away from work. I haven't spoken to my parents or anyone in the family since."

And nobody has tried. I don't know what they tell their friends. Or their church. I stopped hoping for a call after a couple of months went by. Seeing my mother's handwriting brings back the familiar hurt.

"I'm sorry. They shouldn't have done that to you. They are your family. That's supposed to mean something."

I shrug it off. "It means I learned my lesson."

"You should read the card."

"I don't want to."

"Hillary..."

"Fine." I rip it open with shaking fingers, pink glitter puffs out of the envelope. It's your standard sugar and spice welcome to a new girl, along with a check for fifty dollars and an invitation to come by some time.

"They want to meet her." There's this pit in the middle of my stomach that feels like it's sucking everything into it. Like I'm falling into myself and once I'm gone, that's it.

"That's good, right? Mending fences and all that?"

The shudder that wracks my spine says otherwise. No. I can't fall. I have to claw my way back out. For my daughter. "I don't want Kenzie to find out the hard way what happens when you disappoint them somehow. It's better if she never meets them."

I turn and look for something constructive to do. Luckily there are always dishes in my sink that need to be washed.

"Hey." He pulls me into a hug. The spearmint and spice cloud loosens my tension-filled muscles. It feels too good. I want this too much. "I'll go with you."

"What?" I pull back and put distance between us. "Why?"

He recovers quickly, but I see the pain that flashed in his eyes. "Why wouldn't I?"

"I'm sorry, Mac. It's not you. I just don't think it's a good idea." I cross the room and adjust the baby in her swing. "We don't need them."

"Of course you don't need them. But that doesn't mean you can't have them in your life. On your terms." He pulls me over to the couch and sits next to me. "You're the strongest person I know."

"I'm really not."

I miss my parents all the time. It's like a blade making a fresh cut every time when I want to pick up the phone and tell my mom something about Kenzie and remember that I can't. That we aren't family anymore. That they didn't want her or me.

"I know you, Hillary. You will obsess about this if you don't at least try. You'll always wonder if you should have given them a chance. Let's just go and we'll see. If it's a mistake, then you'll know."

"Just go? Like now?"

He stands up. "Like now."

I can think of a thousand reasons not to. And I should go on my own, anyway. Not drag Mac into it. Not depend on him more. But he's right. He does know me, and my mind won't let go. Not after she reached out.

Which is how I find myself on the stoop of my childhood home three hours later. I stare at the doorknob. I can't just walk in anymore. I don't know how to do this. Mac reaches in front of me and presses the doorbell

Right. That's how you do it.

I flex my fingers, curling and uncurling.

"Relax," he says in my ear, that low, gravelly voice that soothes me even when I don't want to be soothed.

"I can't. I feel like my lungs won't expand all the way. This is a bad idea."

Like last night was a bad idea. We still haven't talked about that. How did we get here, on my parent's doorstep, before we talked about the sex we had last night?

Now is not the time to think about sex. Stop it.

The door opens. I don't know why I thought my mom would look different. She looks the same as she did a year ago. It just feels like a lifetime since I've seen her, but it hasn't been one. Her face softens momentarily, then she takes in Mac holding Kenzie in her car seat. "Who in the world are you?"

Mac

I DON'T KNOW WHY I didn't plan what to say to that ahead of time. I should have assumed it would come up, right? Who am I standing on their porch with their daughter and holding their grandchild?

Who am I? Certainly not anyone I currently recognize.

"Mom, this is my neighbor, Mac. He helps me out sometimes."

I'm a cop, and I know how to hold an expression on my face that doesn't go along with what I'm feeling inside. I've had to assure people they were okay when they were not. I've lied to plenty of people to get them to tell me things they don't want to. But as I struggle to hold my cop face in place, my heart cracks like it's been hit with a sledgehammer.

I don't know what I thought I was to Hillary, but *neighbor who helps her out sometimes* wasn't it. Best friend? Lover? Legal father of her child? I shut all that down. I guess it's not important what she tells her parents right now since she doesn't trust them. This isn't a defining moment in our relationship.

Why does it feel like it is?

We enter the house, and Hillary is tense, her expression unforgiving. When her mom wants to hold Kenzie, I can see how much it costs her. Her dad joins us, and he's watching me warily. Who could blame him? This whole situation is weird, and I don't know why I volunteered for it.

I drink my coffee and watch Hillary twist her hands. Small talk is awkward, but since I'm there, nobody gets into the blame game and everyone stays civil.

"When are you going back to work, son?" Mr. Bloom asks me.

"Well, sir. As soon as I'm cleared."

Mrs. Bloom obviously enjoys holding the baby, but she looks up sharply. "You're going back to the ERU? Isn't that dangerous?"

"Mom—"

"Well, isn't it? I would think you might want something safer now."

"Now what, Mom?"

Mrs. Bloom's cheeks pinken. "Well, with you and Kenzie..."

"Hillary and I are just friends, ma'am. You don't have to worry about her getting involved with a cop."

Hillary's eyes cut a path to me, sharp and dangerous. "Exactly. Just friends. Nothing more."

The temperature in the room plummets. Here I thought I'd be a good buffer between Hillary and her parents' tension, but it turns out they have to buffer ours.

I shouldn't have slept with her. How could I not know it would ruin everything? Those hours in her bed were amazing, but it's the months in her life I need more, and I screwed that up by thinking with my cock.

"Excuse me," Hillary says icily as she gets up to use the restroom, leaving me with her folks and a fussy baby.

"Ma'am, may I?" I ask, indicating to Kenzie. Mrs. Bloom doesn't look convinced it's a good idea, but once Kenzie is in my arms, she stops her little cries and settles in.

"You have a way with her," Mr. Bloom says.

"We have an understanding." I shift her to the other arm. "She twists me around her baby pinkie finger and I let her."

Mr. And Mrs. Bloom chuckle and the tension in the room lightens until Hillary returns. I'm not good at emotions, but I can read hers pretty well, and she's pissed and uncomfortable and it's my fault.

I knew I was falling for her. I should have known there would never be such a thing as casual sex when it came to the two of us. Damn. I don't know what she wants from me. When I agree with her that we're just friends, she acts like I'm being an ass. But what am I supposed to do? Shout from the rooftops that I have loved her since the first day I saw her moving in? She is the one who wants to keep it platonic.

This is why I never wanted to get involved. I was fine by myself. I was happy living my bachelor life and not having anyone to answer to.

We don't speak the whole trip back. The meeting went well as far as mending the rift in their family. I don't think it will be easy, but if she and her parents try, I think they can get past it. I know how hurt she is, but I saw the pictures on their mantel. They love their daughter. Parenting just doesn't come with a manual and people are human and screw up.

When we get to the apartment, she stops me before I come in. "I'm really tired. I think I'm going to turn in early. Thanks for the ride to my parents."

The ride? She thinks I went with her so she didn't have to take a bus?

She's got me all knotted up inside. "You want help with Kenzie's bath? I can make you dinner, since you're tired."

The naked longing in her eyes doesn't match her words. "No, thank you. You've been such a good friend to us, but I really don't want to take advantage of you anymore. You should maybe go out, grab a beer with the guys. Have one for me."

Have a beer with the guys? I think I've done that once since I met her. I don't even remember the last time I didn't spend an evening in her living room. "Sure, yeah. Hang out with the guys. Have a good night."

I don't know why she is doing this. Her face doesn't match what she's saying. I could guilt my way in to her house. I could probably even get back in her bed tonight. I'd love to slide back in between her thighs and bury my face in her neck and forget this strange day ever happened. But I can see that she wants to be strong. Sex won't fix this. Not since sex is what screwed it up.

I never should have let myself fall for her. Not when I know I'm so fucked up and she deserves so much more. I think about that as I stare at the white, unadorned walls of my apartment. For the first time, I don't let myself into her house when I hear through the walls that she is up with Kenzie all night.

I don't know what happened to the grumpy fucker I used to be who didn't let anyone too close and who didn't let himself care. It takes everything I have not to break down the wall between our apartments. That's where my life is now.

The life I'm too chickenshit to really live.

Chapter Nine

Hillary

One week later

I JIGGLE THE LOCK ON the mailbox until my key finally comes out. God, I hate these boxes. And this hall. The dingy green carpet smells like moss and tobacco.

"You look like shit."

I squeeze my eyes closed tightly. That is not the thing I want to hear from Mac ever, but especially not after we've gone a week without seeing each other. Despite his words, his voice settles over me like scented bathwater, easing and relaxing everything that's all bunched up inside. How is this a thing? Where does he get this power from? It isn't fair.

"Thanks." I hope my sarcasm came through loud and clear.

"Are you getting any sleep at all?"

I pocket my keys and turn slowly, willing my heart to slow down. It feels an awful lot like standing at my high school locker when a senior I had a crush on asked me if I had notes from class that day. It turns out what he wanted was for me to do his assignment, but I will never forget that feeling of the metal locker behind my back and the object of my affection leaning into me, using all his evil boy powers to turn my insides to mush and legs to jelly.

Are all men devils?

"I sleep some," I answer.

Mac leans down and checks out Kenzie in the baby pack strapped to my chest. Actually, I think he might have just smelled her head.

"She's napping now. Why aren't you napping? That's what the books say to do. You need to take better care of yourself."

Funny thing about napping babies—that's the only time I have to get anything at all done. I decide against snapping off his head, though. He's trying to be nice, I think. "She's been so fussy lately. She sleeps best strapped to me when I'm walking around."

He nods, resigned. I know the Mr. Fix-It in him wants to step in. Make me dinner. Take care of things. He presses his lips together tightly and keeps it to himself.

I'm doing him a favor. He should be out there meeting women and watching sports, not taking care of babies and reluctantly relieving women of their virginity. Okay, he was never really reluctant about it. In fact, he didn't seem to have a problem with fucking me like he owned me.

Now is not the time to let my mind wander to that night. The way he filled me so full that I didn't know where I ended and he began.

Stop it, Hillz. Not only is this line of thought inappropriate, but it's full of bad clichés.

"Do you need anything, Hillary?"

I shake my head quickly. "No, no thank you. We're doing just fine." Without you.

Except we're not. I miss him so much. Kenzie misses him.

But I can't tell him.

His jaw clenches tight. "Okay, well, see you around."

He pushes past me and practically flies out the door onto the street.

This is what is best. Being with him all the time made me weaker. It made me want things. It's better to lose him now than later when he could really tear out my heart. And that of my daughter.

I tell myself this all the way back up to my apartment. The breath is sawing in and out of my throat as I try to hold back the tears. I'm just tired. If I got a good night of sleep, I would see how melodramatic I'm being. He's just a guy.

He's just a *great* guy.

The best guy.

Who am I kidding? He's the *only* guy.

The thought crushes me as I rest my head on my apartment door before I open it. Mac Stryker is the best man I know. I'm hurting him, and he's letting me because that is the kind of man he is. He won't push for what he wants. Not that what he wants is me, but I know that our friendship was comforting to him. I gave him someone to save when he was feeling pretty low.

That's all.

I need to get into my apartment. The tears are already blurring my vision.

"You had me fooled."

I gasp and whirl around, surprised to find him standing right behind me.

"How long have you been standing there?" Why does he seem to have a knack for finding me crying in the hall outside my apartment?

"How long have you been crying over me?"

I wipe my face with the back of my hand. "You know better than anyone that I cry too much when I'm tired. I'm not crying over you—"

He takes two steps and frames my face in his hands. "Here all week I thought you just turned off your feelings. Didn't want me around anymore. I wondered how you could do it so easily. But you're crying over me."

"I'm not—"

He crushes his lips over mine, though he's careful not to smoosh the baby between us. I fight the onslaught for about, oh, .02 seconds, and then I give in. He angles his head, deepening the kiss. He tastes like coffee and spearmint and something else. Something addictive and as good for me as it is bad for me.

I cling to his shirt and whimper into the kiss.

"I've missed you so much," he says, moving down to suck on my neck, nipping my earlobe. Then he leans in and takes a big whiff of the baby's head. I knew it. He was smelling her earlier.

I don't know how to fight feelings for a man who smells my baby's head. I don't think I can. "I guess we should talk."

His penetrating gaze makes my knees weak. "I guess we should."

"We haven't in over a week. It's been hard. I should have...I don't know why I didn't..."

"Okay," he says simply. "I should have too."

"I want to take a shower," I blurt out, because of course I do. I always blurt things out in front of him. I don't know why thinking first is such a problem. "I mean I want to take a shower before we talk. I feel...well, the baby threw up. On me, as usual. As I'm sure you can smell. And I just feel like before we talk I should clean up and get my bearings. Maybe then I'll stop rambling also. But I make no promises."

Mac snorts but refrains from laughing out loud. "I'll take Kenzie. You take a shower. Then we'll talk."

The way he says *talk* sends the blood in my veins to sizzling. *Down, girl.*

"Right," I say breathlessly. "Talk."

Of course, as my life goes, two hours, one shower, one more throw up, some hastily eaten cheese crackers and we still haven't talked. But he's bouncing an almost sleeping Kenzie around on his chest, and I've changed my shirt and hidden all my dirty clothes under the bed in case our talk ends up in there eventually. That's about as good as I can expect things to get right now.

I think of the life I thought I would be leading just a little over a year ago. I was going to be a career girl. I wanted to work downtown and own a penthouse apartment and date fabulous men in suits while I ate expensive caviar and drank some kind of signature cocktail I'd yet to decide on. Something old fashioned, I thought. Something Ingrid Bergman would sip.

Instead, I smell like puke. I rarely sleep. I don't converse with adults often. I drink fake wine. I'm in love with an out-of-work cop who doesn't know it and a two-month-old tyrant who pulls my hair when I profess my undying love to her.

I wouldn't trade a minute of it.

But I need to handle the cop situation.

"She's asleep." He gets her in the crib without waking her. "Maybe I should tell you to go to sleep too. You might need rest more than—"

"Please don't go."

He looks like I just punched him in the gut. "All right."

"Sit, please." I gesture to the couch. I join him, though it's not like it used to be, when the space between us didn't seem too likely to zap us like an electric fence if we didn't leave enough room. I inhale and exhale slowly. We're both sitting up with great posture staring ahead at...well, nothing. But I can see our reflection in the black screen of the television. We look like two people who've never met.

I need to say something. "So, we had sex."

Long pause.

"Yep. We did." His words come out gravelly, like it's been a long time since he's spoken.

Long pause.

"It was my first time, but as far as I could tell, it was pretty much...mind-blowing."

Long pause.

"Yep."

Long pause.

"Well, good talk." I start to get up, but his arm shoots in front of me and I settle back in.

"This is ridiculous," he says. "What are we doing? This is *us*. You and me. People live their whole lives wishing for the relationship we had before we even had mind-blowing sex, and now we're acting like uncomfortable strangers. And I hate it."

"I think I'm so afraid of losing you that I'm going to lose you."

"Please, Hillary. Look at me, not the floor, me." I slowly turn to find his gaze. "You will never lose me."

My blood is roaring in my ears. "I want to trust you. I really do. You've done nothing but be wonderful to me since we met, but I'm damaged."

"You're not damaged."

"I am. I spent my whole life thinking life was safe, and then in one week, I learned I couldn't trust the two people who were supposed to love me no matter what. I didn't enjoy being dumped by the asshole, but it was nothing like being dumped by my family. And then you came along and were perfect and I'm afraid to ask life for what I want because now I have so much more to lose." My gaze flicks across the room. "So much more."

He takes my hand. "I'm not perfect. I'm a fucking disaster. And I don't trust myself, so I guess I can't figure out why I think you should. But I want you to. I want you to trust me and I want Kenzie to trust me. And the two of you are the only things I want. And I don't feel like I deserve you. But I want you. Hillary, I love you."

All the air is knocked out of me. "Like a friend loves a friend."

"Yes."

Mac

SHE STARTS PULLING into herself. "Like a friend loves a friend. And a man loves a woman," I say quickly. Shit. Trust me to screw this up. I fucking hate feelings. Shit. "I love you in every way. I have never felt this way before. And I have no idea what I'm doing."

Hillary lets out a watery laugh. "I have no idea what I'm doing either."

My throat is thick with feeling. I can't believe I said it. It was like cutting the last wire on an explosive. Now that it's out there, done, and nothing exploded, I don't know what to do with myself. "I talked about you at my group meeting this week," I confess.

"You did? The same group where you usually don't talk at all?"

"Yeah. It was the first time I opened up to those assholes about anything, and they told me to stop being a pussy and tell you how I feel."

Her eyebrows meet above her nose. "That's an interesting therapy group you have."

"They were right. I should have just told you last week when I woke up that the nightmare was the same one I've been having since the bomb killed Ricky. Instead, I tried to act normal, failed, and made you think I was ghosting on you. I have PTSD, and I'm sure you already know that, but I didn't want to tell you. I like being someone you rely on and I was..." Damn, I hate feelings. "I was scared that if you saw how raw I am, you wouldn't feel safe with me. And so, I ended up somehow making you feel unsafe with me anyway."

She nods. "Okay, but then instead of telling you to stop ghosting, I let my anxiety about trusting people win and talked myself into thinking that it would be better to not let you get close again, so I started pushing you away."

"So we were both being dumbasses."

"Basically." She reaches her hand out and grabs mine. "I'm so sorry you still dream about that explosion."

"I'm sorry I'm not the guy who tells you shit you need to know about how I'm feeling." Look at that. I did it. I said stuff. Important stuff. And the world didn't end.

"So we're communicating now? I can tell you anything?" she asks.

"Of course you can."

"Okay, then I should tell you that I really, really liked having sex with you."

I squeeze her hand, remembering her moans and the way she came, squeezing around me so hot and so wet. My dick gets instahard. "Yeah, that much I already know. You were a wildcat in there."

She punches my arm. "I'm being serious. It was worth waiting for. Even if I ended up having a baby before I had sex for the first time."

"We should do it again sometime. But none of that friends with benefits bullshit. This is the real deal for me, Hillz."

She bites her lip and looks at the front door like she wants to bolt. "I'm still insecure."

I push the hair that has escaped the elastic band off her face. "I'm still fucked in the head."

She gets this little smile like she knows a secret, a womanly secret. I understand that Mona Lisa painting people talk about a whole lot more now. When a woman gets that smile when she's looking at you, you know what it means to be a man.

"When you said you thought we should bang again, did you mean tonight? Because I'm willing to skip the tiny houses marathon if you have some more things you'd like to show me."

Fuck me. My cock is rock hard and ready. But part of me, the asshole, remembers she's been up all night all by herself the last few nights. "You need to sleep."

She swings her legs over my lap and wiggles her cute little toes. "I'd rather get laid."

My mouth waters remembering the way she tastes, and all my nerves are on high alert waiting to feel her skin against mine. But no. "I've heard the two of you over here the last two nights. You need to rest."

"You're no fun." Her feet move over my cock, rubbing it through my pants. "I'll sleep later."

It's tempting. God, it's tempting. But she's got purple skin under her eyes, and she yawns every two minutes. I have to push her legs back to the floor so I don't jump her. "I'm going to make you dinner and then you are going to sleep. When the baby wakes up, you can feed her, then I'm taking her back, and you are going back to sleep."

She groans when I get up.

"Kraft?"

"God, no. If I never have macaroni and cheese again, it will be too soon."

I wonder if she'll change her mind the next time she's pregnant. I can't fucking wait to find out.

Holy shit. I want to get her pregnant.

I want it all.

It occurs to me that she didn't tell me she loves me back.

Chapter Ten

Hillary

TRUE TO HIS WORD, MAC did make me sleep last night. And I'm grateful, really. But damn, all day I've been thinking about tonight, and I can't tell if I'm more nervous than horny or the other way around.

I'm in the bedroom when I hear the front door open. I take a deep breath and one last look in the mirror. Here goes nothing.

I pause in the doorway and wait for him to notice me.

He looks up from the newspaper he'd brought in with him and his mouth goes slack. Then a slow smile builds across his face. "Wow," he says in a voice that sounds deeper than usual. "You look...wow."

I let out the breath I'd been holding. "Thanks." Wow is exactly what I was going for.

I will myself not to trip as I enter the room the rest of the way. I haven't worn heels in a long time, and these are particularly precarious, but also make my legs look miles longer than normal. I hope my hips are swaying sexily, and I'm not actually loping strangely as I walk.

Finding a dress in my closet that still fits was also a challenge. I'm rounder everywhere than I used to be, but I have to say my tits look amazing even if the dress can barely hold them. I just need to not breathe very much. It will be fine. I'm sure of it.

I hope.

Mac is staring and swallowing hard, his Adam's apple doing double-time. That's good, right? He opens his mouth, then closes it, then opens it again before he says, "Are you going out? I thought we were having dinner here?"

I laugh. "We are. I just wanted to make it feel special." I try to cover the growing wistfulness in my voice. "You've never seen me in anything but pajamas and sweats."

"That's not true. There was the gown...you wore in the hospital."

"Ha-ha."

He saw me naked, too, but we're circling that territory very carefully, it seems.

He's having a hard time keeping his gaze off my boobs, so I guess the dress is working. And also I could have skipped the heels and he wouldn't notice. He's not looking at my legs at all.

"I feel under-dressed. You look so pretty, and I'm wearing jeans. Should I go—"

"No! I just wanted to..." Oh my God. Am I about to cry? Please tell me I am not about to cry. Why am I crying?

This sucks. When am I ever going to get my own emotions back from hormonal overload?

"Hillz?"

I wave my hand. "I'm fine. I don't even know what's upsetting me. I just feel like you've been so great, and you deserve to have someone pretty and who at least tries to impress you, and I used to be better at the glamour stuff."

He gently pushes my hair off my face. "Baby, you don't have to impress me with pretty clothes. You've got me on the line already, remember?"

I sniffle. "I just wonder if we had met differently, like in a club on a Saturday night...I just wanted to make sure I would have caught your eye."

"First of all, I didn't go to clubs before we met, so I never would have seen you. Second, you caught my eye before we met. I avoided you for a couple months after that."

"I did...wait...you avoided me?" What is this new and interesting information?

He sniffs the air. "Are you cooking?"

"Sort of. Don't change the subject." I go into the kitchen and open the oven where the takeout is keeping warm. "I couldn't cook and spend most of the day trying to get ready for this date, so you get rigatoni from Mama's."

"I love the rigatoni from Mama's."

"I know, duh. That's why I ordered it." I start dishing us up. "Now why did you avoid me?" I'm dying to know.

"Because I was attracted to you and I didn't want to be."

"Why?"

"Well, you were packing." He makes a round gesture over his stomach. "I didn't know if you had a boyfriend or husband. And...I knew you were too good for me. You're like sunshine, and I live under heavy clouds."

Sunshine. He thinks I'm sunshine. And he's wanted me for a long time. And what the hell am I afraid of?

I kick my shoes off across the room and march right up to him, framing his face in my hands. "I want you to know something."

"What?"

"I love you, Mac Stryker. I wanted to make tonight special so I could tell you and wow you with my pretty dress and the makeup and I even brushed my hair. I don't know if you've seen me with brushed hair in the last two months. And I still want tonight to be special, but I did all this because part of me was scared that if I didn't make it special, I wouldn't be enough. But when I look at you, really look at you, I know I don't need to be scared. I feel your love, and I hope I can make you feel the same."

"I love you." He pulls me into his body. "I love you so damned much."

He kisses me, and I realize dinner is going to wait.

Of course, Kenzie starts crying. He touches my forehead with his. "We'll pick this up again when she goes back down."

I nod. I'm going to have to change out of the dress first, since it's not nursing friendly.

Such is my life.

Mac

MY BALLS ARE FUCKING the bluest blue ever. Kenzie is having a rough night, and I feel bad for the kid, but I'm near the end of my own rope.

We took turns eating a cold dinner standing up at the counter. Hillary is back in her flannel sleep pants and nursing tank top, her hair back in its messy knot. Long gone is the siren in the little black dress and stiletto heels. And while I appreciate the image of her standing in that doorway practically falling out of that dress that hugged her in all the right places, I'm just as turned on by the vixen in plaid pajamas.

Turned the fuck on.

I take advantage of a chance meeting in front of the fridge when neither of us have a baby in our arms. My lips find the back of her neck, and I plant soft, tender kisses from the base of her neck slowly up behind her ear. She gasps and presses into me, gasping again at the rock-hard dick in my pants.

"Soon, baby." God, please let it be soon. The only thing I want is to bury myself balls deep in her slick core. And her mouth. And God help me, her ass.

I spin her to face me, looking deep in her eyes right before I lock my mouth with hers. My tongue traces her lips slowly, and her hips press against mine. She comes alive suddenly, plunging her tongue into my mouth, exploring and sucking on my lips, pressing and rubbing her tits against me. I growl, grabbing handfuls of ass and grinding my hard dick into her body. "You're being a very naughty girl." I bite her neck lightly.

She writhes in my arms, reaching with one hand to hold the back of my neck, holding me in place. "I want to be so much naughtier."

I growl before I let her go. I have to, or I'll fuck her right here, right now. And tonight should be special, not a quick fuck against her fridge.

Later, Kenzie finally loses some steam and some of whatever baby angst is keeping her so fretful. I take her from Hillary's arms and put her in her crib. I love this kid. I didn't know I liked babies. But this one, this one I like a lot. I kiss her as she snuffles into sleep.

A quiet falls over the apartment like a sigh of relief.

Hillary wraps her arms around my waist, her breasts cushioning me from behind. "I don't know what I would do without you, Mac."

"Let's agree never to find out." I turn so I can hold her. Hillary is too young for me. Too sweet for me. Too good and funny and sexy. But none of that matters. "You're it for me. You know that, right? This isn't one of those *let's see how this works* things. This is for real. Forever."

"Forever?" Panic darts across her face. She's not sure she trusts the word forever. I'll just keep showing her until she believes me.

"Forfuckingever," I say and start walking her backwards to the bedroom. I close the door and turn her into it, shoving her back against it. I pull her shirt off roughly, checking her eyes to make sure I shouldn't be more gentle. All is I see is heat. It's the fire of passion. Of need. I know instinctively what she needs from me. I always have. And it isn't gentle and sweet lovemaking. My woman needs to dance close to the flames.

I sucked at her tits, softly biting them, then come up and growl in her ear. "You need this, don't you?" I suck her earlobe. "You need me."

"Yesss." She grinds her hips against my aching, hard cock.

"You." I grip her pajama pants and pull them down forcefully. "Are." I completely rip off her panties. "Mine."

She moans. Fuck. I feel like an animal. My cock is straining against my jeans. I kiss her again. Bite her neck. Kiss her collarbone. I press her higher against the door and her legs wrap around my waist so I can grind my cock against the entrance of her pussy.

"Whose are you?"

"Yours," she answers with no hesitation. "I'm yours."

"Mine," I growl and suck on her earlobe again.

She tugs the shirt out of my jeans, and I shrug it off onto the floor, kissing her deeply, my tongue thrusting in and out of her mouth. Fucking her mouth the way I want to with my cock.

I have enough sense to pull a condom out of my pocket while she's undoing my pants. "Someday, we're going to do this raw. I'm going to fill you up with my come."

She fumbles with my zipper and stares into my eyes. "If we do that, I might get pregnant."

"Oh, you'll get fucking pregnant." I finish getting the rubber on because she looks too dazed. "Kenzie needs a brother or sister someday, and I fucking love your body when it's pregnant." I position the head of my dick on the mound of her slick pussy. "I told you forever, and I meant it, Hillz." I ease in slowly and her tight channel eases around me like a glove. "I'm going to give you everything I have. My love, my name, my babies."

"Your dick. Right now, I just want your dick."

"Naughty girl." I tighten my grip around her hips and moved her higher up the door to fuck her better. I pull almost all the way out, slowly, and move slowly back in. My thrusts are mercilessly slow. Thorough. Deliberate. She starts moving her hips against mine, faster, gyrating greedily as I torture us with my pace. "You're so tight. So good."

I get my hand between us and thumb on her clit. That's when she starts going crazy.

"You like that, sweetheart?" Her pussy clenches violently around my cock. "Oh, you do. Are you going to come on my cock?" I growl and fuck her harder. Faster. She's whimpering, her body convulsing with need. "Come for me, you dirty, dirty girl."

She flies apart in my arms, her pussy clenching and milking my dick. So beautiful. I'm barely holding on, but I don't want to come yet. I want to watch her soar.

Her body starts trembling and fuck if mine isn't shaking too. I somehow step out of my pants without toppling us to the floor and grip her ass tight as I take her over the bed. She opens her eyes, a little surprised to find herself lying down.

"Oh, we're just getting started, sweetheart."

Hillary

HE SMILES SLOWLY, SEDUCTIVELY, his eyes dark and dangerous. "I'm going to wring every ounce of pleasure out of your hot little body tonight. I promise." He pulls my legs over his shoulders as he lunges toward my pussy. I'm sopping wet and the sound of his mouth on me is obscene.

I like obscene.

His tongue circles my clit...over and over he circles it, stopping occasionally to fuck me with his tongue. He sucks my lips into his mouth and laps up my juices thirstily, almost savagely, groaning about how good I taste.

I begin to whimper. It's too much, this onslaught of pleasure. He takes two fingers and plunges them deep inside me while he sucks and licks and makes love to my pussy with his mouth. I can't control myself, the noises I make. The way I beg.

"Come on my tongue, Hillary," he commands.

And I do. I shatter into a million pieces, my body twisting, my mind spiraling. My body is wracked with wave after wave of pleasure, my heart beating through my chest.

"You are so beautiful." His voice is guttural, thick with lust above me. I can hear him, but he sounds so far away. My body is limp, but in the fog, I realize he still hasn't come.

He grabs my ankles and bends my legs to my shoulders before he slides into me. He's thrusting deep, not so controlled now. His hard, hard cock fills me. I can feel him everywhere in my body. Beads of sweat have formed on his brow, and his eyes are wild. He's like a Greek god towering above me, so masculine and strong. All his muscles gleaming with a sheen of sweat.

"I love you, Mac."

He pauses, his eyes darkening as his pupils dilate. The air around the bed fills with static like right before a storm. He lets go with a groan that is wrenched out of him like it's painful.

His hips thrust down like he can't help it, making me take more of his straining cock than I thought I could. Deeper, harder. I can feel the coiled need wound tight in his cock, in his whole body. Tension vibrates through his thighs, and his powerful grip on my flesh hurts just the right amount.

"Yeah, take it, take that fucking cock. You feel so good. Make me come." He strains upward, his entire body clenched and gripped in that rising tension before surrender. He starts bucking hard, and his mammoth body is shaking all around me. His body jerks as he comes, his breath ragged, his face screwed up tightly.

I bury my face in his neck and gyrate against him as another orgasm wracks me with pleasure.

He collapses on top of me and I clutch him as tightly as I can, loving the weight of him. The smell of him. We're exhausted and sweaty and the air around us is filled with the scent of sex. He rolls over, pulling me with him so I'm on his chest instead of him on mine.

"Jesus." He kisses my head. "That was amazing."

My heart is slowing finally. "Yeah."

"Hillz?"

"Hmmm?"

"When we wake up, we don't get to act weird. This is the new normal. I love you. You love me. If you get scared, you have to promise you'll tell me."

I settle into his arms, his heartbeat under my head. A fleeting thought nags at me. He talked about marriage and babies earlier. But as fast as it flits through my head, it's gone, replaced by slumber.

Chapter Eleven

Mac

Two months later

I HAND COLD BEERS TO Cap and Cafferty and look around at all the shit in the living room of my new apartment. I don't know where the hell it's all going to go. Box towers are leaning precariously all over the place. Mostly books. Turns out Hillary had a storage unit full of books in the basement of our old building. "Thanks for helping, guys. Don't suppose you want to stay and help unpack all this?"

Cap pats me hard on the back. "We're happy to see you settled. She's a great girl. You're on your own with the unpacking."

"She's got to be a fucking saint to put up with your bullshit," Cafferty says. "But I'm happy for you man. Also, not staying."

Cap laughs, that big booming sound I've missed. "So, you start your new gig on Monday, Stryker? Should I bring you an apple?"

I take a long pull from the beer. "Can you picture it? Me an instructor?" I clench my right hand as much as I can. It's clear I'll never be back on bomb tech. I'm not even cleared for weapons since I don't have the control I need with all the messed up tendons and bone fragments. But as long as I continue to check in with my psych appointments, Cap was able to get me in as an instructor at the academy.

Hillary comes out of the nursery with her dad. Things are still tense, but he asked if he could help put together the crib, so we invited him over. Everyone is taking baby steps. I'll still check his handiwork, though. Turns out I'm kind of an overprotective dad. Never saw that coming. The overprotective or the dad part.

I check on the munchkin in her swing. She likes watching everyone move the furniture around. We're all here for her entertainment, I think.

As always, my gaze seeks out Kenzie's mom. Something's off with Hillary's body language today. Her movements are jerky, and she's only half paying attention when people are talking to her. She didn't seem that bothered by her dad asking to help the other day, so I'm not sure what changed her mind. Maybe it's just moving. It's a big step.

I suppose I could have made it more romantic. My exact words were, "We could save money paying for one apartment instead of two since I only go home to get more clothes."

I wonder if that's what it is. Maybe she's wishing I'd made a bigger deal out of it. Maybe she's worried about my level of commitment. Maybe I should stop wondering and just ask her. Those are the rules now. We talk. We say what we mean. And I have to share my feelings even when my first instinct is to pretend I don't have any.

Fuck, but I hate feelings talks.

The guys clear out. Mr. Bloom leaves. Hillary puts Kenzie down for a nap. I pace, mentally trying to have the conversation with her so I don't screw it up.

When she comes out of the baby's room, she closes the door softly behind her. "Wow, I really like having a second bedroom. It will be nice to have all the baby stuff out of the living room."

She smiles, but it doesn't light up her face like her real ones do. Shit. She isn't changing her mind, is she? I take a deep breath.

"We need to talk," we both say at the same time.

"Babe, is something wrong? When you're not wringing your hands, you're playing with the hem of your shirt."

She drops her hands to her sides like I just challenged her. "Having a relationship with a cop is hard. You see too much." She points to the couch. "Sit. I have something for you."

I push shit onto the floor in case she wants to sit next to me. Where are we going to put all this stuff? I didn't think I had that much, but when you move two apartments into one, it's way more than we need. Maybe I can learn to build some bookshelves or something.

She comes out of the bedroom with a gift bag, which she thrusts at me. "Here."

"It's not my birthday. Are we having an anniversary or something?" She's not been the "it's our one-month anniversary of the first time we ate pizza together" kind of girlfriend, but maybe I've been missing the signs of necessary romance.

"No. It's just a gift. Open it."

I'm nervous, but I don't know why. "Does this have something to do with why you've been distracted today?"

"Will you just open the damn bag already?"

I hold my hands up. "Okay, okay." Jesus. I pull out the tissue paper first. She used a lot of it. Inside the gift bag is a box of Kraft Macaroni and Cheese Dinner. "Uh, thanks, babe." I have no freakin' clue why she would give me a box of...wait a minute.

She's chewing the inside of her lip watching me very closely.

"You said you didn't like this stuff anymore." My voice sounds a little accusatory. I don't mean it to, but my mind is sparking off in too many directions at once.

"I know."

"Are you by any chance craving it?"

Her eyes get watery. "Don't be mad, okay?"

Mad? "Babe—"

"I don't know why I'm such a freak of nature. We used a condom every time. I'm just obviously a very, very fertile person. I mean, considering how Kenzie got here, I don't suppose we should be surprised, but I can't think of a single time when we weren't careful. And I know this is not a great time. You're starting a new job and we just moved in together and are getting used to being a family. Daycare is going to wipe out my savings if the diaper costs don't do it first. And we haven't talked much about the future since we're just getting used to the now and—"

She's pregnant? I pull her onto my lap. "Are you going to let me talk ever?"

"I ramble sometimes."

"I noticed." I cup her gorgeous face in my hands, stunned like I am every day that she's mine. "We're having another baby?"

She dips her face into my neck and inhales. "You're not mad, are you?"

"Do I look mad?"

Hillary pulls back and looks at my face. "No. I'm a little mad. Why aren't you mad?"

"I'm concerned. Kenzie's birth almost took you away from me. Do you think it's safe to have another baby?"

"My OB told me at my last appointment that I could still have more children. They would probably treat my pregnancy as high risk, but there would be no reason to assume the same thing would happen."

"Okay, but nobody thought it would happen so soon. You need to go see a doctor right away. You haven't already, have you?"

She shakes her head. "No. I just got a test from the drugstore." She sighs and curls up a little more into me. "You're sure you're not mad?"

"Sweetheart, you and Kenzie are the best thing that ever happened to me. You know that. I love being with you."

"Don't think I haven't heard you trying to teach her to say da-da every time I leave the room."

"You mad?"

"No, it made me cry, though, knowing you wanted to be her daddy. That was the first clue that my hormones were out of whack again. I'd been getting better about not crying at everything, and then I got sideswiped with a craving for macaroni again."

"As far as I'm concerned, as far as anyone is concerned, she's my daughter. You know that, right?" We never did anything about my name on the birth certificate, so I'll never have to adopt her. She's already mine.

"I love you."

"God, I love you too." Another baby. My life is so different from even less than a year ago.

It begins with a sweet hug and then a tender kiss but, like always, it quickly turns to more. The kisses get deeper, our tongues dancing, darting in and out, testing and teasing. A light nibble here and there. Our hands begin exploring as we settle into the couch. I cup her breast and her hand cups me lower, feeling how firm and wanting I already am. Always. My fingers wrap in her hair and pull her closer. Her hips rock almost lazily. Just a bit of a grind.

My hand edges the fabric of her shirt, slowly inching underneath. Our bodies continue to rock to meet one another, pulling closer, deeper. I lean in and smell the crook of her neck, kissing her skin and feeling the muscles beneath it tighten. Her breath quickens. She's my whole world, and I uncover her bit by bit. Her shirt. My shirt. My mouth never stops kissing her as we undress. Her pants. My pants.

She straddles my lap, naked and grinding that sweet pussy against my aching dick. She's so wet. Always ready for me. I angle my cock, and poise there, pausing to take in the look on her face when I first slide into her. It's my favorite moment—the anticipation for when the head of my thick cock slips inside her, pushing her, stretching her.

"Look at me." She opens her eyes. "Good girl." I slide the thick head of my dick through her creamy cleft and push inside, burying my cock deep inside her and watching the first shock of my entry on her face. Then the arousal.

She gets lost in me. Every time. There's nothing like it. She told me once I become her sun when we fuck. The rhythm and stroke of my throbbing cock becomes her heartbeat. That she goes somewhere only

I can take her when I'm inside her. Remembering her words, knowing she's mine, completely mine, right now makes me swell more. I fuck her deeper, harder, and she sucks me inside her body.

I hold her hips and angle mine, watching my cock disappear inside her. "Ride me, sweetheart."

She throws her head back, arching in sweet abandon. Up and down, harder and harder. "Fuck...fuck...you're so deep inside me."

"It feels so good to fuck you raw, Hillary. I'm going to fill you up with my come."

"Yes," she whimpers, nearly begging. "I'm yours..."

I can't stop grunting like an animal as she rides me hard. I start thrusting like a desperate man. "Such a hot, tight pussy," I pant in time with my thrusts.

Her limbs start to seize. "Look at me," I demand as I grab her chin. "Look at me when you come." I slow, giving her long thrusts until she starts contracting around me. Then I pump into her while she rides out the waves of pleasure crashing over her. Her warm, slick juices drip down my dick. I'm never wearing a fucking condom again. This is amazing.

"Keep coming all over me, babe. I love that sweet pussy so much," I urge in her ear as I wrap my arms around her tightly. "I'm going to come inside you...deep inside you...fill you up."

I can't stop it now. My body tenses into a free fall of ecstasy. My balls tingle and I shoot deep, spurting into her trembling body as I quake uncontrollably, pouring everything I am into the woman I love.

She collapses onto my chest, and we are still for a moment, our lungs sawing for air. Heaven. She's heaven on earth.

I squeeze her. Probably too tight. "Please marry me."

I should have planned it better. Gotten a ring. Flowers. A babysitter.

Instead, we're covered in sex in the middle of boxes and newspaper. I'm still inside her, and she's still shaking from aftershocks. My timing is not great.

I don't care. "Please," I repeat.

"I suppose I need to make an honest man of you. Especially if we end up with the same maternity ward nurses who already think we're married."

"So that's a yes?"

Kenzie's cry punctuates the room from the baby monitor.

Hillary laughs. "I'll marry you. I'll marry you every day for the rest of your life if you want."

Epilogue

Hillary

Five years later

I'M FEELING...WELL, I don't even know how I'm feeling. I just finished my very last final exam and am now officially done with my degree in advertising. I thought I would feel really excited or relieved or happy or something, but I just feel like I checked off a box on my to-do list.

A nine-year to-do list, but it's still anticlimactic.

Mac asked me to stop at Old Joe's on my way home and pick up his debit card that he dropped on the floor that morning. It's a little weird. Mac is not the guy that loses his debit card. Not like me who lost my keys the first day we met.

I suppose I should be thankful I'm such a mess. It got me the guy, right? I figure the man who met me with cankles but still found me attractive is a keeper. I have pretty good ankles now, I must say. I don't work out as much as I should, but I give it more effort than I used to. Mostly because Mac insisted on the self-defense class which led to me actually enjoying hitting and kicking things. Who knew? Now we have bags in the basement for my hitting and kicking pleasure.

I almost forget to stop at Old Joe's. I'm making more lists in my head. What I need at the grocery store for one. I think it's my night to cook dinner. I'm almost sure of it. Maybe I'll get a double shot of something before I leave. It's rare that I don't need a jolt of caffeine. I pull open the door expecting to hear the bell above it jingle. Instead, I hear, "Surprise!"

The banner above the register says, "Congratulations, Hillary!" Standing in front of the counter are Mac, my parents, Joe, Cap, our neighbors, and my sweet daughters, Kenzie and Ricki. Well, okay, they aren't really all that sweet. Every now and then they are, though.

I immediately tear up and then mentally count the days since my last period while everyone hugs me. No, I'm good. Tears of happiness, not tears of hormonalness. I love our kids, but I am not ready for a third.

"Mommy," Kenzie hands me her artwork. "I made this at school today for you."

I clutch it to my chest and give everyone hugs and kisses. "Thank you, everyone, for being here. I couldn't have gotten my degree without all of you."

I catch the eye of my husband. *Especially you*, I tell him with my eyes.

I have zero clue what I'm actually going to do with this degree. I've spent the last few years concentrating on small children, and Ricki isn't in school yet, so I'm not going to start work until they are both full-time. But I finished it. That was the important part.

Mac slides his arm around my waist when we find a small pocket of privacy. "So proud of you, babe," he says into my neck.

Instant goose bumps. Still After all these years.

I turn in his arms. "I'm glad to be done. Now, I'll have more free time in the evenings, after the girls go to bed." I press my boobs into his chest. "I need a new hobby. Any ideas?"

He looks down my shirt. "I have a few."

"Yeah?"

"Yeah. You can watch the games with me. Basketball is your favorite, right?"

I wince. Not basketball. He still wants to watch it all the time and it still annoys the hell out of me. "Funny. I was thinking something more active, maybe."

"Yeah?"

"Yeah. Maybe we could buy one of those Kama Sutra books and try a new position every night."

I feel him harden against my stomach. "That's better than basketball."

We have our coffee and cake and go home. I stop for takeout instead of groceries.

Our house is small, sometimes it feels even smaller than our last apartment, but it's got a small yard and it's close to the schools. I remember worrying how I was going to raise my daughter alone, now I never have to face anything alone.

After dinner and baths and storytime, I take a long bath myself. When I'm boneless and relaxed, I decide tonight is an excellent night to try something new.

I slide into bed next to my husband and grab the remote to turn off whatever ESPN show he was engrossed in. He gives me a look and a pinched expression.

"You will be happy I did that. Trust me."

He blows air out his nostrils, but his curiosity is piqued when I open the nightstand drawer and toss a bottle of lube in front of him. Up goes his eyebrow.

"Really?"

I nod.

Mac kisses me, his tongue probing, his lips sucking. We've been close to going in the backdoor several times, but I always chicken out. Tonight, I'm up for adventure.

I tug his shirt. "I want your skin, Stryker."

He gives a slow, graceful smile, and I feel bits of my heart bloom. "So take what you want, baby."

I undress us both slowly, and he watches intently. "I love the way you're looking at me right now."

"I love looking at you."

I swipe my hand across his chest and down, his muscles jump reflexively under my hands. "I love touching you, too." My hands continue to rove over the mountains and valleys of his cut torso, the soft, downy happy trail showing me the way to where I want to be.

I smell the hollow of his throat. Mine. He's mine. He was made for me.

He wrestles me under him, and I pretend to fight him off, my resistance a turn-on to us both. I want to take and be taken.

We're kissing and the heat, the longing, and the need in his eyes, makes me so wet. "I got you, now," he says.

"I guess you do. The question is, what are you going to do about it?"

"Always need to challenge me, don't you?" A dimple flashes and he bites my nipple.

I arch into him. My body is humming at his promise. I'm up for everything. I want his hot, wet mouth. I want his dick inside me. I want *everything*.

He moves up to the head of the bed, straddling me. His dick is thick and heavy, sprouting proudly from a dark nest of curls. He's leaking with desire, the tip of him glistening. He feeds it to me slowly. I love the taste of him. The silk of his dick on my tongue.

"Oh, baby. You're going to make me come too fast like this. And I want your ass tonight." He pulls himself away and crawls back down the bed, lowering his face. "This pussy. Fuck."

The licks, the sucks, the kisses to my pussy and the tight rim of our next frontier are not controlled. My husband is feasting on me, and the noises he's making are clearly those of a happy man.

He moves up my body until we're face to face. The look in his eyes is calculating as fuck. "I'm going to fuck you now, baby." His lays his cock against me so I feel its girth, its length. He picks up the lube. "You sure about this?"

I nod as he prepares his giant cock with lube. I'm nervous but excited. I get on my hands and knees. His cockhead presses against my ass, and then he pushes in slow and holds there, kissing my spine. I stretch around him, a little pain mixed in with the pleasure. I can feel every inch of him as he works it into me. Nerves I didn't know I had tingle and zap. I turn to look over my shoulder and watch his face as he watches where we are joined. He's trying so hard to keep that feral animal inside him controlled, but each second is harder than the next for him.

He takes it slow and lets me get used to him, inch by inch. I clench my jaw and gasp, feeling him work that fat cock deeper into me. My husband always feels so big and solid. I'm intensely full.

He hisses with pleasure when his balls finally slap against my pussy. He's all the way in now. Dull discomfort mixes with pleasure inside me. He withdraws, and I get a second of relief. Another thrust. Gradually, I can feel him picking up the pace, and a pleasurable pain radiates out from my center.

"You're so tight. You feel amazing." He rides me harder and adds his hand to my pussy, rubbing my clit. The things he does with his fingers makes me see stars. "You're so wet, naughty girl," he says. "Your sweet pussy is so tight and hot and wet on my fingers. And your ass is squeezing me so tight."

It's too much. All the sensations are overwhelming. "Finish me," I plead. "God, please."

"Baby, I thought you'd never fucking ask." He grinds his pelvis into me, and he uses his thumb on my clit, hard.

Light flashes behind my eyes as I come, clenching hard on his dick. It's raw. Pure. Untamed. Mac roars, that animal finally let out of his cage, and he pumps more and more into my body.

When he collapses on the pillow next to me, neither of us know what to say. So, we start to laugh.

"Jesus. That was amazing. I love you so much. Are you okay? Did it hurt?"

I snuggle into him. "A little. The good kind of hurt though. Tell me that again tomorrow when I try to sit down though."

We clean up and get a snack, watch some TV, and as I drift off to sleep, I realize that my life just keeps getting better every day. That the secret is trusting him. Trusting love. And saying what I feel. That's all I have to do.

Tomorrow is another day. I promised Ricki we could make cookies when her sister goes to school. I should probably clean the bathrooms—things slid a lot during finals. Maybe I can get out of cooking dinner tomorrow, though, if I suggest we BBQ. Mac likes to think he's some kind of gourmet at the grill, and I let him because it makes him happy, and it's less work for me.

He curls around me in his sleep, pressing my back into his chest.

Yeah, I'm glad my life exploded into such mess five years ago. My heart got pretty banged up and bruised, but it makes it all the sweeter now.

About the Author

LIKE FIRST TIMES? FORBIDDEN fruit?

Yes, please.

Love a hot, dominant alpha claiming what's his?

Heck, yeah.

Want to watch him fall hard for the sweetest fantasy he didn't know he needed?

Me too!

I'm Brill Harper and I love happily ever afters, smokin' hot bad boys, and quirky heroines that I'd love to be friends with off page. These ladies are not perfect—but they're perfect for one man—and he's always sexy AF.

Seriously—these heroes only have one weakness, and it's sticky, sweet love. They don't let anything stand in the way of taking what belongs to them. When it comes to the woman they love, it's hard cocks, dirty talk, and soft, mushy heart feels. I like to call them Alphamallows.

* Brill Harper is a pseudonym. Like...a secret identity. By day she's Clark Kent, writing romance books for young adults and grownups. By night, she's Brill Harper writing unfailingly filthy, yet super sweet books, that would make her alter ego blush.

Brill Harper is represented by Deidre Knight of The Knight Agency.

Visit me on Bookbub[1]

---

1. https://www.bookbub.com/authors/brill-harper

Did you love *Banged*? Then you should read *Tapped: A Blue Collar Bad Boy Book*[2] by Brill Harper!

Anker Beck is just doing his time tapping kegs at the neighborhood pub while he socks away money for his dream: to own his own brewery. What he doesn't have time for are relationships, but not being interested seems to make the women in the bar want him more.

That's when *she* starts coming in. Mousy, plump Annabelle Rogers, roommate of his co-worker. She brings her books to the pub and seems to do everything she can to stay invisible. So why does he keep noticing her?

One night, when a female patron is getting particularly handsy with him, he tells everyone that Annabelle is his girlfriend and kisses her in front of the whole bar. She has every right to be mad, but the

2. https://books2read.com/u/3krVVO

3. https://books2read.com/u/3krVVO

mousy girl surprises him with a challenge: She'll pretend to be his girlfriend to keep the women away if he agrees to help her with one little thing: losing her virginity.

With a catch.

He absolutely isn't allowed to fall in love with her.

Author Confession: It's a role reversal for the bartender to give the customer *the tip*, isn't it? There's also tapping, dry hopping, and some thick foamy head—it is a bar after all. But do you really think I could write an alphamallow who doesn't fall head over heels for the mousy, plump girl? I think you all know me better than that by now. Let's hear it for BBW love and blue collar heroes!

Read more at https://brillharper.com.

Also by Brill Harper

It's Complicated
All Together
All at Once

Love in Brazen Bay
Wrong Number Text
The Right Stuff
So Wrong It's Right
Don't Get Me Wrong

Standalone
Dirty Jobs: a Blue Collar Bad Boys Collection
Notch on His Bedpost
Honeymoon With The Prince: A Royal Romance
Good Girl

Watch for more at https://brillharper.com.